# The Ranger's Texas Proposal

## Jessica Keller

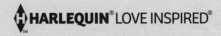
HARLEQUIN® LOVE INSPIRED®

Special thanks and acknowledgment are given to Jessica Keller for her contribution to the Lone Star Cowboy League: Boys Ranch miniseries.

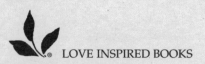

PLEASE RECYCLE · THIS PRODUCT IS RECYCLABLE ·

Recycling programs for this product may not exist in your area.

LOVE INSPIRED BOOKS

ISBN-13: 978-0-373-71987-7

The Ranger's Texas Proposal

Copyright © 2016 by Harlequin Books S.A.

www.Harlequin.com

**Printed in U.S.A.**

May the God of hope fill you with all joy and peace as you trust in Him, so that you may overflow with hope by the power of the Holy Spirit.
—*Romans* 15:13

Dedicated in memory of those who made the ultimate sacrifice in the line of duty. To the guardians of peace and civilization. The heroes.

Our thanks and honor will never be enough, but it's yours.

# Chapter One

"A forced vacation," Heath Grayson grumbled and tightened his grip on the steering wheel. He loathed speaking on his phone through his car speakers. It felt unnatural.

"You need time off. You won't take it. Where does that leave me?" Chuck, the major who oversaw the Texas Rangers out of Company F, was starting to lose his patience.

"It leaves you with a man who wants to work. Why not just let me keep working?"

"Rules are rules, Ranger. The handbook says I'm not supposed to let you carry more than one hundred and sixty vacation hours into the next year."

"I know this is only the start of my second year as a Ranger, but the Department of Public Safety hasn't ever enforced that on me." He'd carried hundreds of vacation hours with him when he became a Texas Ranger. Hours he'd never used during his years working in the investigative unit of the state troopers. "My paycheck comes from them. We're still under their umbrella."

"Unfortunately, the Ranger unit is a little stricter

with time usage. Now…even if you stay away all of November—which I'm ordering you to do, hear me?— you'll still be carrying over four hundred hours into next year. I can't believe they let you bring that time with you when we hired you."

"It's all the same branch of the government." He tried to keep the grumble out of his voice this time but wasn't successful.

"I'm aware of that. But the Austin office is going to mince me if you don't start whittling these hours away."

"Fine. Sorry. I don't want to cause you any trouble. I'll stay away." Heath swallowed hard. Worked his jaw. Still, after all these years, why was it so hard to talk about it? "But do I have your permission to look into that cold-case file we talked about…on my time?"

Chuck sighed. "I won't stop you from looking into your father's murder, if that's what you're asking. But, Heath?"

He glanced down into the footwell on the passenger's side of his truck, where a box of file copies on his dad's murder rested. "Yes, sir?"

"That case has been cold for fifteen years. Arctic cold."

Heath sucked in a breath. "I'm well aware of that, sir."

Fifteen years.

Heath had now been without his father for just as many years as he'd known the man. The hero. The Texas Ranger who had lost his life on the job. Heath had followed in his father's footsteps—at least in choosing the same profession. Heath tapped his badge, resting in the compartment near the driveshaft. However, he wouldn't make the same mistakes his father had. Heath wouldn't get married. Wouldn't drag kids into a situation where they might lose their dad like he and his sister had. He couldn't do that to people he cared about.

Chuck cleared his throat and Heath got the sense that the major was about to try to talk him out of his mission, but instead he said, "Best of luck, and rest up. That last case… You've done a lot of good, son. I wish we had more awards to hand you for that one."

Heath dragged his hand over his short dark hair. The last case had worked him raw. "I don't want awards. That's not why I do this job."

"All the same. There are twelve kids out there safe today because of your work these past few months. Allow yourself a moment to celebrate that while you're enjoying vacation. For me. That's an order."

"Will do, sir."

Heath had been the lead Ranger on a statewide bust that had started as a drug-smuggling investigation but blew up to uncover a dirty underground of child trafficking. It took months of covert and often stomach-turning investigation, but Heath and a few other officers had been able to bring charges against the seven top guys in the criminal ring. They'd arrested six more on lesser offenses. And twelve kids had been set free. He'd never forget their faces when he broke into the room and ushered them to safety.

That was why he did this job, even though it was inherently dangerous. Bringing about justice, seeing people free and safe again…that was why he wore the badge.

And now he had one more kid to help out. His teenage self. Ever since his father's murder, there had been a weight, a binding around his chest. If he could close the case, perhaps he could move past the anger that still bubbled inside that boy who'd lost his dad. The boy who'd fought with his dad the last time he saw him. The boy who'd never gotten to tell his hero *I'm sorry* or *I love you* one last time.

Which was why he was keeping his vacation local. Haven, Texas…home of the boys ranch where his father had been murdered.

First, though, he had to investigate some mischief that had been occurring at the boys ranch, where his buddy Flint Rawlings now worked. Flint had asked him to look into a string of minor offenses. Not exactly normal Ranger-type work, but Heath was desperate for an excuse to plant himself in the middle of the boys ranch in order to poke around about his father's case anyway. He'd investigate some calves getting out of their pens and some petty thefts if it served that purpose. Besides, Flint and Heath had been friends since basic training, back when they'd both served as soldiers. Heath wasn't one to turn his back on the few friends who had stuck with him over the years.

Heath adjusted his visor, blocking the midmorning sun from blazing directly into his eyes.

Flint had explained that the troubles at the ranch had escalated last night. A female volunteer by the name of Josie Markham had witnessed someone running out of the barn, calves following in the person's wake. No one knew how the perpetrator broke into the barn. But they had a firsthand account from a witness, so at least there was a starting point.

More than Heath had to go on about his father.

Was the mischief at the boys ranch a coincidence? Doubtful. At the moment, Heath would guess everything amounted to pranks or the frustrated acting out of a disgruntled resident. It was a home for troubled boys after all. But Heath wasn't a guessing sort of man. He believed in hard facts and logic. Everything had an answer if a person was willing to dig far enough to find it.

He'd built his life on information and facts, and currently Josie Markham was in possession of both those things.

Josie Markham took a deep breath as she stopped for a moment to lean against her late-model truck. Morning sunlight traced through the unkempt field behind her home. Next year she'd plant something there. This little patch of land would be a working ranch with crops, too. She clenched her fists. No matter what, she was determined to see her dream through.

"I can do this." She rubbed her hands over her arms, trying to warm up.

Even in Texas, early November mornings carried a chill. A shiver raced down her spine, but it could have more to do with exhaustion than the weather. Josie sighed.

There wouldn't be time to relax today.

The animals needed to be cared for, she had to make something to eat, and by the time those things were done, she'd have to head to the boys ranch across town for her volunteer shift. Bea—the director at the boys ranch—had already urged Josie to begin cutting down her hours serving there, but she didn't want to. As a new member of The Lone Star Cowboy League, the organization that ran the boys ranch, Josie felt a responsibility to be there whenever she could. But it was more than that; Josie loved working at the boys ranch. She thrived on the animal-husbandry classes she taught and the hours she spent in her role as mother's helper inside the large home on the property.

Chores. She needed to finish her chores before she could think about anything else.

Josie started to move, but then decided to allow herself the small luxury of one more minute watching the sunrise before heading into the barn. Fingertips of sunlight outlined the stable and a fenced-in pasture area. Golden and pink light sketched into the fleeing night sky, making the world glow with possibility.

If Josie lived to be a hundred, she'd never get over the beauty that was the rise and fall of the sun each day. A reminder that everything had a beginning and an end—a marked-out time—that she had no control over. But God did. He knew and nothing happened outside of His care. Didn't the Bible say there was a time for everything? A time to cry, to laugh, to rejoice. God was in control.

Some days she almost believed that.

Josie traced her fingers over the large dent and scratches along the side of her truck; most of the bronze paint had started to peel off in that area. It didn't look pretty, but she wasn't going to waste money fixing it. Not that she would have had the money even if it desperately did need to be fixed.

When they'd purchased the truck as newlyweds, Dale had often kidded her that the bronze clashed with her auburn hair. Foolish man. He never did understand what the word *clash* meant in a fashion sense. She shook her head, suppressing the smile that pulled on her lips whenever she thought about their early days together. The good times.

*Don't think about Dale. Don't cry.*

Her throat clamped and she blinked back the burn in her eyes. Texas dust. That was all it was. The dust.

After paying off the gambling debts and back taxes she'd discovered after Dale's funeral, she'd had to sell their home and most of their married belongings. All but the truck—she got to keep it because it was paid off. The vehicle was all she had left of her and Dale's life together.

Her hands automatically dropped to her expanding midsection.

The little person growing and moving inside of her begged to differ about the truck being the only piece of their marriage left. Tears found their way to her chin. The irony of her situation—almost six months pregnant and a husband buried just less than that—tore at her heart. The week before he was gunned down on the job, Dale had started packing to leave her. He'd wanted a son—a child—and in ten years of marriage, Josie hadn't gotten pregnant.

She hadn't been enough to keep Dale happy.

Now none of that mattered. He was gone and they were having a child. A child she'd raise on nothing. With no husband, no man to help with chores or bring in a paycheck or hold her when she wanted to fall apart and cry.

For the rest of her life…alone.

"We're going to be okay, lima bean." Her voice broke on the nickname. "Hear that?" She rubbed her belly. "Don't mind your mama's tears here and there. The doctor tells me that's all part of being pregnant. Emotions. Lots of 'em. So don't let them worry you at all.

They don't mean anything. You and me are going to be just fine."

If she kept repeating that, maybe it'd be true.

Heath glanced at the screen on his GPS. Almost there.

Over the phone, Flint had given him the name Josie Markham along with her address and sent Heath off to "go along, now, and do your investigating." Knowing Flint, Heath was fairly certain the man hadn't given Ms. Markham a heads-up that a Ranger was on his way over. No matter. It wouldn't be the first time he'd shown up at someone's home unannounced, and it sure wouldn't be the last. It went with the job.

Wind whipped through his windows, carrying the scent of dirt and cattle and something musty—stale water. Decay. A low river. They'd had a dry summer and not much more rain so far that fall, either. Later in the day, the high would sit in the upper sixties. Cold by Texan standards, but Heath liked the fresh air. He'd always choose fresh air over the vented stuff.

Heath pulled onto a small dirt road, dust swirling behind his truck. At the end of the road, the ranch that greeted him left something to be desired. Could it even be called a ranch? A small cabin perched on the edge of a meandering river. Cattails encircled the opposite side of the water from the cabin and there was a tiny dock, good for launching a rowboat or canoe. It would also make an ideal fishing spot. Too bad Heath wasn't much of a fisherman.

There was a large SUV-type truck parked beside the cabin. It sported a dent almost big enough for a person to hide in along the passenger side. No way that door opened anymore. Recent crash? The lack of rust said so. Was someone still driving around in that thing? It couldn't be safe.

Behind the cabin was a barn that had seen better days. Heath parked his truck, stepped out and ducked past the cabin to get a better view of the rest of the land. Scratch his original thought—the barn had seen *much* better days. The thing looked liable to fall down in any stiff wind, probably smashing whatever poor animals called that place home in the process.

Right when Heath was about to turn toward the cabin, he spotted a petite woman coming out of the barn, struggling as she huffed and puffed behind a creaking wheelbarrow.

His long stride ate up the distance quickly. "Here. Let me help."

The woman set down the handles, balanced the wheelbarrow in the soft earth near a grassless pen and swiped sweat from her forehead. One of her fingers poked through a hole in her worn-out work gloves. The nail polish on it was chipped, but purple. Her hair color fell somewhere between red and brown. She had it pulled up, but it must be long to make that gigantic bun on her head. He never understood how women were able to get it to look that way, all piled on top... Didn't it hurt? Wasn't that much hair heavy?

The woman—Josie Markham, according to Flint— set her hands on her hips and scowled at him as if Heath were a spider on her wall. "What can I do for you, Officer?" Her tone said she didn't really want to do anything for him. Ever.

He raised his eyebrows.

She heaved a sigh. Her cheeks were flushed from

exertion. She grabbed at the collar of the light green shirt she wore, fanning it to cool herself down. "White hat. Boots. White starched shirt. And that belt's the type they only issue to Texas Rangers." She gestured toward his holster. "I hope you weren't trying to be undercover."

"Good eye." He extended his hand. She narrowed her gaze but shook it. "Heath Grayson. I'm a friend of Flint's."

In the space of a heartbeat, her hesitant expression vanished and was replaced by wide-eyed concern. "Did something else happen at the ranch?" Her lips parted to suck in air and her skin went paler than it was naturally a moment ago. Josie had one of those the rare types of faces that didn't age—she'd look young forever. Even though she was probably nearing thirty, she could pass for eighteen.

She shifted from around the wheelbarrow. "What are we waiting for? If something's wrong, let's go." She started toward her truck.

Once she moved away from the wheelbarrow, he saw her stomach. Pregnant. Very pregnant. That fact wasn't a maybe or a possibly—it was a certainty. Flint had mentioned Josie was widowed, but he'd left out the little detail that she was with child. So, a recent widow.

Had she been in the barn alone...doing chores?

Heath imagined his sister, Nell. She'd been married to a fireman a few years back. Bill. A loser. He'd cheated on Nell and left her alone, pregnant with their daughter, Carly. Even the reminder of the man caused Heath's hands to bunch into fists. Heath had always wanted to march up to Bill and give him a piece of his mind, but Nell had forbidden any such nonsense. His younger sister was a strong, determined woman. The set of Josie's chin hinted that she might have that in common with Nell.

"Let me help you with your chores," Heath said.

Josie's jaw dropped. "What about the boys ranch?"

"The ranch is fine."

"Why didn't you say so? You about gave me a heart attack." She laid her hand on her chest and took a few deep breaths. Then her eyes skirted back up to capture his. "If the ranch is fine, why exactly are you here, then?"

She fanned her face and dragged in huge amounts of oxygen through her mouth as if she was having a hard time getting it into her lungs.

Now he'd done it. Gone and gotten a pregnant woman all worked up. Did he need to find her a chair? A drink of water? Rush her to the hospital? What a terrible feeling, being out of control. It was disconcerting. With his training as a Ranger and his years as a state trooper before that, he was far too used to knowing what to do in whatever situation he was placed in.

"Are you all right, ma'am?" He took hold of her elbow and steered her away from the barn, toward the cabin. She felt so small and breakable. There wasn't much meat on her arm. "What do you need?"

"I'm fine. Just fine." She laughed. "You should see your face, though." She pointed up at him and covered her mouth, hiding her wide grin. Her warm brown eyes shone with mischief. "Now *you* look like you're the one having a heart attack. Relax there, Officer. It was only a figure of speech." Her laugh was a high sound, full of joy. Josie laughed with her whole self, without holding anything back.

Heath wanted to hear it again.

She even smelled nice—a mixture of sunshine from the outdoors and something sweet, almost like the scent that used to drift through his childhood home when his mom was making caramel chews.

"You still haven't answered my question."

Had she asked him something? Heath scratched his chin.

Josie crossed her arms, resting them on top of her protruding stomach. "So, then, Heath Grayson, Texas Ranger, what brings you to my ranch?"

He toed his boot into the parched earth. How on earth was this tiny woman making him feel as if he was the one under questioning, not the other way around? Off-kilter. That was the way to describe how he felt.

"Flint wants me to speak with you about the incident last night. About the calves."

"Funny." She inclined her head. "I didn't take this for something that required the intervention of the Texas Rangers."

"You're right. This isn't exactly official business." He made finger quotes around the last two words. "I'm on vacation. Only doing Flint a favor."

"Ah, so you're a do-gooder, then? The married-to-the-job type. Poking around for petty criminals on your off time?" The tug of her lips let him know she was teasing him again.

Silence usually worked when he was locked in a room with his worst offenders. Perhaps the trick would get the firecracker that was Josie Markham to stay on track, as well. Heath locked his jaw out of habit.

"Okay. I see. That's your confession look." She pointed at his face. "That's the stern one that gets the bad guys to give in. Fine. Be that way." She pulled off her gloves and wiped her hands on the thighs of her jeans. "Well, let's get it over with quickly, then. I've got a lot that needs to get done today." She jutted her thumb over her shoulder, pointing at the barn.

Heath's gaze traced back over the patched-together ranch. If Josie was all alone, she needed help. That should take precedence over an investigation about some loose cows. It wasn't exactly like anyone was in immediate danger. Not from what Flint had shared.

Unlike the danger that had plagued the boys ranch fifteen years ago.

"How about I go ahead and help with your chores first?" Heath crossed his arms and widened his stance, ready for the fight he was sure this woman would put up. He'd spent enough time on his uncle's ranch over the years, especially after his father's death, that Heath knew his way around a barn and wasn't shy when it came to manual labor. He was just as much at home mucking stables as he was on the shooting range.

Her lips pinched as if she'd bitten into something sour. "Absolutely not."

No one could say he wasn't a good judge of character.

"I insist."

Josie blew out a long stream of air. "Listen, Officer Grayson—"

"Heath is just fine." He took a half step closer.

"Heath, then." She patted her hair. "I make it a point not to spend too much time around lawmen anymore."

*Anymore?*

"Interesting." He held his ground. "We're at an impasse, then, because I make it a point not to leave pregnant women on their own to do any heavy labor."

"*Labor*, really?" A muscle twitching on her cheek said she was fighting the upward tilt of her lips. "That's the word you're going with?"

"Let me help you. Please?" He softened his voice.

Why was he pushing this issue so hard? He didn't know Josie, but her condition twisted his gut and it tugged at him… She could be Nell. He'd been with the state troopers, stationed clear across the state when Nell fell on hard times. The distance had made it impossible to help her at all when she was alone and pregnant with his niece, Carly. Heath would always regret not being there for them. But perhaps lessening Josie's load—if only for a month—could be a small way to atone.

Besides, she was a witness to a recent crime. Even though Flint didn't believe there was an immediate threat, depending on what Heath's investigation uncovered, it could mean Josie was a target. Especially if she had been seen or if her information led to someone's capture.

He couldn't leave her on her own.

Heath had a month off… Why not help around her ranch? He needed something to do with his time and he wouldn't be able to spend every second of his vacation at the boys ranch investigating his father's murder. Not without people becoming suspicious. He didn't want them all to know that was what he was doing there. There was a chance he'd solve nothing. That he'd fail. He definitely didn't want them to feel sorry for him, the way people often did when they found out about his father's death.

Helping take care of Josie gave him an out…an alibi. He could help on her ranch and then drive her—because her truck was not safe in its current condition—to the boys ranch for her volunteer hours, which would give him a believable reason to hang around so much. Because he knew Flint would get annoyed if Heath trailed him around at the ranch. Hopefully, Josie wouldn't.

He yanked off his hat and laid it over his heart. "My mother would be ashamed of me if I left your ranch without pitching in. Say yes…for my mother's sake."

Josie popped her fists onto her hips and let out another loud laugh. "Well, if you're going to guilt me by bringing your mom into things, I guess a girl's going to have to accept your help." She shook her finger at him. "But mark it in the books that I am accepting begrudgingly and slightly under protest."

"Under protest." Now Heath was the one who couldn't help but smile. He wasn't used to that. "I'll be sure to mark that down."

The woman was definitely a bit of a spitfire. And not even an inch of her was intimidated by his being a Texas Ranger, which was refreshing. The instant respect that often came with the office was nice, but it tended to keep everyone at an arm's distance.

Heath rolled up his sleeves and got to work.

This November, Josie Markham wouldn't be alone. Not like Nell had been.

Not if Heath had anything to do with it.

# Chapter Two

At first Josie followed Heath around. "My ranch may look like a mess. I know it does. But I'm only starting out. This has been mine for the last five months. I haven't had time to turn this place into what I've envisioned. But I will."

Heath nodded. "I'm certain you will."

He moved the cows out of the barn and into the pasture. After the cows were cleared out, he wrangled the three large hogs into a separate penned area, away from the cattle. The man spent an hour mucking out the stables and refreshing them with clean straw. While he worked, Josie minded the chickens, hunted for eggs and milked her dairy cows along with the two goats that rounded out her animals. Heath lunged for the metal buckets when Josie made a move to lug them toward her house.

"I got them." He scooted over and made a grab for the pails.

"I'm perfectly capable of bringing them in, Officer Grayson."

"Heath. And while I know you're capable…remember… my dear old mother." He winked at her.

She rolled her eyes, but moved out of his way. "Fine, then. Follow me, *Heath*."

"Lead the way." Heath grabbed the pails and inclined his head. "I'll follow you wherever."

*I'll follow you.* He'd meant it about the pails, but the words made her heart speed up just the same. Foolishness. Josie had only ever dated Dale, and Dale didn't believe in chasing a woman in order to win her. She'd never been followed…pursued. Not when they were dating and definitely not after they had married. Dale had referred to romance as a "mind game."

But as Josie made her way toward the cabin with Heath trailing her, the Ranger's hard-won smile and teasing wink flashed through her mind.

Oh, this was bad. Very bad. Mayday bad.

Most mistakes started in the form of a good-looking man.

She peeked a glance at him over her shoulder.

Definitely a mistake.

In those leg-hugging jeans, boots and with his sleeves rolled up until they were snug around his tanned forearms, the man was far, far too handsome for his own good. And when he'd taken off his hat and invoked his mom, his almost-black hair, messy and sticking out at weird angles from wearing the hat, about did her in.

Josie had always been attracted to the tall, dark and handsome type. Heath Grayson definitely fit the bill. He had dark, wide eyebrows, and his eyes were black coffee—hold the cream.

Don't forget tall. The man had a foot on her, maybe more.

Josie had met her late husband, Dale, when they were

in high school, and they'd started dating soon after. He'd never grown beyond the five foot seven he was when they'd met. And Dale's face had been rounder—softer around his edges. Whereas Heath had sharp lines, as if his face had been chiseled from stone by some great, ancient artist.

She shook her head, releasing her wayward thoughts.

There was zero reason to compare the two men. None whatsoever. So they were both in law enforcement? Big whoop. That didn't mean she needed to pull out a chart and make a pros-and-cons list of whom she was more attracted to. Goodness... Dale was her husband. *Her husband.* At least, he had been her husband and he hadn't passed away that long ago. She was still working through the grief of losing her first love, losing the man who would have been the father to the child kicking in her stomach.

The attraction she felt for Heath—a man she'd only just met—had to be her pregnancy hormones talking. The doctor had said her emotions would do silly things in the next few months leading up to the birth. That must be the reason for her rapid heart palpitations, and the way her gaze kept tabs on Heath all morning and memorized the way his dress shirt pulled across his shoulders... It was crazy pregnancy stuff. End of story.

Besides, Heath Grayson was a lawman. Not just any lawman—he was an officer who worked the most dangerous and high-stakes cases in the state. A Texas Ranger. If Dale, who had been a sheriff's deputy, could die in the line of duty, Josie imagined the target on a Ranger's back was even bigger.

Especially these days.

Her front porch made a horrible moaning sound

under their combined weight and Josie grimaced. The old fishing cabin had belonged to her father and had fallen completely out of use after his passing several years ago. Dad had left it to her, and Dale hadn't wanted to care for the property. Once she'd moved out of her and Dale's old home, the fishing cabin was all she had to her name. She'd been proud of the little space. It was hers. One hundred percent hers. It was the first time ever that she'd lived alone, which she discovered she didn't like, but that was a different issue altogether. The fact was, now she knew.

But for as much pride as she had in the small patch of land that she was trying to turn into a functioning ranch and the tiny two-bedroom cabin that was going to be the perfect amount of space for her and her baby, worry lanced through her. She tried to see the place through Heath's eyes. Would he consider it shabby? Think her poor and tragic?

Josie lifted her shoulders, filled her lungs and held up her chin as she opened the door. This was her home. She refused to care what anyone else thought about it. She was determined to craft this cabin into a welcoming place filled with love. One her baby would enjoy growing up in. She wouldn't waste worry on what a passing-through Texas Ranger thought. No matter how much the muscles in his arms popped when he carried in her milk pails.

Josie stepped around Heath and opened up her green secondhand refrigerator. "Just set them in the bottom there."

He did so and then turned to face her, almost as if he was waiting for her to issue his next marching orders. She couldn't allow him to work on her ranch for a few hours and then send him on his way. That wasn't good manners. Besides, she still needed to fill him in about the incident she'd witnessed at the boys ranch.

Josie clasped her hands. "Why don't you wash up and have a seat? After that many chores, I have a feeling you've worked up an appetite." She rubbed her palms together, hesitant. Was this a good idea? Too late. "Bathroom's the second door in the hall there."

"Ma'am, there's no need—"

She held up her finger in that scolding way she used to do when she worked as a nanny years ago. "Ah. I won't hear it. Now's my chance to invoke *my* mother on you. She wouldn't hear of me sending away an honest, hardworking man without so much as offering a scrambled egg or two, so I won't listen to any arguments. Scrub your hands and have a seat."

"Yes, ma'am." He tipped his hat.

"And no more *ma'am* stuff," she called after him as he made his way to the washroom. "I'm probably younger than you are."

"I'm sure you are," he called back.

Josie mentally cataloged what ingredients she had and settled on biscuits and gravy with a side of cheesy scrambled eggs. She'd made a batch of her favorite biscuits from scratch the other night and there were plenty left over. They were always a huge hit when she shared them at the boys ranch. She popped a bunch of them onto a pan and set her oven to warm.

After she wiggled the knob on the stovetop, it finally clicked and the flame went on. She set a skillet over the flame and crumbled breakfast sausage into the pan. Grease sizzled and popped. Josie licked her lips. She was hungry and loved cooking. These days, though, she often skipped making what she considered real meals because there was only her.

Making food for one was no fun.

She scraped the skillet and then sprinkled in the flour, keeping an eye on it while the grease soaked it all up. Next the milk and then the rest of the flour and seasonings. The mixture would have to be stirred frequently now so it didn't get too thick or burn on the bottom. Josie juggled cracking the eggs and starting to scramble them along with stirring the gravy with finesse.

When breakfast—she glanced at the clock and saw that it was ten in the morning, so it was closer to brunch now—was done, she arranged both their plates and then turned toward the table. Heath sat there, his hat off and resting on the pole on the back of his chair. His dark hair was doing that adorable messy, sticking-up thing again. Josie tried not to stare, but it was hard not to.

"That bad?" Heath's cheeks reddened and he patted his head. "Should I put the hat back on?" He swiveled around to grab the Stetson.

He had noticed her staring? How embarrassing.

Josie swallowed hard and forced her eyes down to their plates. "No. You're fine like that. Just fine." She set the plate with double the amount of food in front of him and then took her seat across the table. "Would you mind saying grace?"

"Of course." Heath nodded and bowed his head. "Father, we thank You for the people we meet and the adventures You take us on. Bless Josie and her baby, keep them both in good health. Bless this food to our bodies, that we'll use the energy to go out and do things that glorify You. And bless our conversation. In the name of Your Son, Jesus, we ask all these things. Amen."

"Amen," Josie whispered. "Thank you."

"Sure." Heath shrugged and gave her a look that said it was strange to thank someone for saying a prayer. They both dug into their food. Heath passed a compliment her way after every bite.

"I haven't eaten that well in..." He leaned back and rested his hands on his abs. "Well, suffice it to say it's been a long time since this bachelor has had a good meal. I don't think I've ever used the oven back at my apartment for anything beyond frozen pizza."

Living off frozen pizza? Josie shivered at the thought. "No Mrs. Grayson, then?"

"There's my mother?" He shook his head. "But no, she hasn't been Mrs. Grayson in fourteen or so years. She's Mrs. Nye these days."

"Dating?" Why was she grilling him?

"No, ma'am. I'm not exactly the dating type."

She pointed her fork at him. "What did I say about the *ma'am* business?"

He ran his hand over his hair. "Force of habit, I'm afraid." Then he rocked forward, pushed his plate to the side and rested his hands on the table. "How about you tell me what happened at the barn last night—go ahead and go into detail, if you will."

"Right." Josie clasped her hands in her lap. "It was just past sunset last night. I know that because the boys were in the dining room with their house parents—there are couples at the ranch who serve as counselors and role models for the boys living there. They had just finished dinner. I was heading out to my truck."

"That one out there?" He jutted his thumb toward her driveway.

"The only one I have."

He laid a hand on the table, giving off a relaxed air that Josie knew—from Dale's training—was all part of the tricks of the trade when it came to getting a witness to feel comfortable in an interview. "Is it safe to drive?"

"Is this pertinent to my story?"

"No." He shifted in his seat. "I apologize. Continue, please."

"Well, I was about to unlock my truck but I froze because I heard a clanging sound, and I know that sound because it's very distinct. I hear it every day." Josie stopped clenching her hands together. *Relax.* She wasn't on trial. Heath was here to help.

She took a deep breath and continued, "It was the side door to the calf barn. The one I personally had locked before dinner. I'd asked one of the ranch hands— Davy—to grease the door so it wouldn't frighten the calves anymore, but I guess he hadn't gotten around to doing that yet. Good thing, too, because if he had, I might not have seen all of this and the calves would be lost."

"You're positive it was locked?"

"Absolutely. I sent the boys in to wash up for dinner and I stayed back and locked all the doors before I headed in."

"So you heard the door open?" he prompted.

"Yes, and then I saw someone charge out of the barn."

"Could you describe them?"

Of course he'd ask that. She should have used the

past few hours to try to draw a better, clearer image from her memory.

She shrugged. "Medium height, medium build. I'm sorry...that's all I've got." She blew out some air. "They were wearing a hooded sweatshirt and it was dark out. I never got to see his face."

"His? Are you certain it was a man?"

Questions... Josie took a deep breath. It was Heath's job to pick apart her story. That was how he found the truth. Josie knew that, but even still, it made her want to shrink. Dale had never been able to turn off his police brain. He spoke to Josie the same way he would a suspect. Maybe that was an across-the-board thing for all people in law enforcement.

She picked at a chip in her table. "I guess I'm assuming that part."

"Do you have any idea who it might have been?"

"No. I mean, at first I thought it might be one of the older teens from the ranch. They have setbacks sometimes. But it wasn't one of them."

His chair creaked. "You're positive?"

"Absolutely. They wouldn't do something to put the calves in harm's way. Even if one of them were upset."

"Did the person recognize you?"

"No. Maybe? How would I know? I didn't recognize them. But I talked... I said my name." She licked her lips, remembering that detail. She'd called out to the person... *It's Josie.* If one of the boys had been in distress, she'd wanted to be able to help them.

Heath leaned forward.

Josie pressed on. "The person took off toward the open pasture and I couldn't chase them." She gestured toward her abdomen. Pregnant women didn't run. Hopefully, Heath picked up on that without her stating it. "And as they took off, all the calves spilled out of the barn and started running around the ranch—into the darkness. I couldn't catch them all, so I called for help and all the boys and the house parents came out and helped corral the calves. We caught them all and were finally able to locate all the boys, too."

"Locate the boys?" His head tilted, just by a fraction. "So someone was missing?"

"Stephen." Should she have told Heath? She didn't want him to grill the teen. Stephen had been aloof recently, but he was still on track to go home next month. "He's seventeen. But he's a good kid. He didn't do it."

"How can you be certain?"

"He had a book with him. He'd been out reading."

Heath frowned. "Outside? In the dark?"

"It wasn't him."

Heath's brow dived. He used his pointer finger to rub under his chin. "How long were you outside before this all happened? Roughly."

"Fifteen…maybe twenty minutes maximum."

"Alone?" His eyebrows inched closer together with each question. "What were you doing out there for so long?"

She'd been focusing on how lonely she was. She'd been crying, not looking forward to the quiet back at her cabin. She'd foolishly asked God for a second chance at life and love.

Josie hid her shaking hands under the table. "Does that matter to the case?"

"It might."

*Calm down.* "I was thinking. Thinking and watching the sunset. That's all."

He touched the tips of his fingers together. "I ask because I have to determine the suspect's most probable time of entry into the barn. You didn't hear someone accessing the barn before then?"

"Not at all. I'm the one who locked it. All the doors were locked. And that was at least an hour before then."

Heath rocked forward. "More than likely the perpetrator was camped inside already when you locked the doors."

"He was in there with me?" That idea made her skin crawl. She'd locked up alone and it wasn't like she walked around the boys ranch armed.

"That's my guess. It could change depending on other information." He leaned back in his chair again and tapped one finger on the table a few times. "Then again, it's most likely one of the boys, so there was probably no danger."

"It wasn't one of the boys. They were all accounted for." *Besides Stephen, but it wasn't him.*

Heath pressed back from the table and crossed his arms. Leveled her a doubtful look. "Those boys are at that ranch because they're trouble. They wouldn't be there if they weren't. I wouldn't put it past any of them to cause problems. They've done worse."

Josie pressed back from the table. How could Heath say those things? Peg the boys as bad eggs before he'd even met them? Was he one of those cops who had seen so many horrible things that he automatically assumed the worst about everyone? She had watched Dale grow bitter about the world, more so each year on the job.

She shouldn't press Heath. Then again, Josie had promised herself after Dale passed away that she wouldn't allow anyone to push her around ever again. Not that

Heath was being pushy. But from now on, she was going to be strong. Ask questions. The old Josie always swallowed her thoughts and opinions… No longer.

A breath. "I'm sorry, but your tone. You…you don't like them—the boys—do you?"

"I don't know them. I've only been to the ranch a few times and last time was years ago at the old location."

"Yet you're judging the boys anyway." She shouldn't be talking to him like this. Heath was almost a stranger, and here she was challenging him. But it grated on her to hear someone misjudge them, and so quickly. The Lone Star Cowboy League had worked hard to try to weed out the rumors in town that the boys at the ranch were trouble, yet still some of that belief lingered.

Heath scooped his hat off the back of the chair and worked it around in his hand. "See, that's where people get it wrong, though. Using good judgment isn't the same thing as being judgmental."

A fire lit in Josie. She wanted Heath to see the boys differently. But how to do that? "How long are you around, doing this favor for Flint?"

"For November."

She had a month to change his opinion, and she knew just how to do it. "You should volunteer at the ranch. Get to know the boys." It would be good for him. Besides, the boys would be floored if a big, important Texas Ranger started hanging around them.

Heath's eyebrows formed a V. "Why?"

*Think like a lawman… What will convince him?*

She took a deep breath. "For starters, your presence will prevent anything else from happening. Also, if you really think it's one of them, that'll put you in close proximity. You'll be able to get to know them and talk to them. Someone might even confess. Or you may see that they're wonderful and realize you were wrong to judge them."

Heath rubbed his thumb over his nose. "You know what, that's not a half-bad idea. It would help my... investigation. You're right about that. I'll talk to Flint about it tomorrow."

Josie's heart tripped over itself at the thought of spending more time with Heath. Of course she wanted him to change his opinion about the boys, and time at the ranch was the best way for that to happen. But what if it changed her opinion about men in law enforcement?

Her eyes skirted over the lines of his strong jaw, his shoulders. He'd given up so much time to help her this morning and he hadn't talked down to her at all. Maybe he wasn't like Dale. Maybe...

The baby inside of her moved, rolled. Josie loved that feeling. She hugged her stomach. Above everything, she had to protect her child from hurt. That was her duty as a mother.

No lawmen.

If God did choose to give her a second chance at love, He'd have to bring a nice insurance agent or IT man her way. Someone who worked a boring, safe job all day, tucked away behind a desk. One whose greatest career danger was an ink stain.

Not someone who carried a gun for a living.

# Chapter Three

The loud noise outside sent Josie reaching for the closest heavy object.

A frying pan.

She pulled back the curtain over her sink and peered outside. Heath's large Ford pickup was parked near the river, dwarfing her vehicle. He'd unlatched and opened the barn—which explained the noise—and had already headed inside. A minute later he was leading out the cattle.

"That man," she grumbled and set the pan back onto the stove. "What is he up to?"

He'd left soon after their brunch yesterday. Said even though his apartment was only forty-five minutes away, he needed to check into the Blue Bonnet Inn in town because he preferred to stay close during an investigation. He explained that if something happened at the boys ranch, he wanted Flint to be able to call him and be only minutes away. Which made sense. Flint's place at the boys ranch wasn't that big and his young son lived with him—so asking Flint to host him for a month, even though Heath and Flint were close friends, was probably asking too much.

Josie had to chuckle, though. The Blue Bonnet Inn was an upscale place inside an old historical home. The rooms were decorated to match Texas flowers. It was better suited for a granny on vacation than a lawman. Heath Grayson would stick out there like a rooster in a henhouse.

She rested her elbows on the counter and cupped her chin in her hands. Today she'd have to ask Flint exactly how long his friend was going to stick around and be a pest in Haven. Heath had given her the vague answer of November, but she had a hard time believing that an investigation into a few missing items, a lost therapy horse last month and the calf incident would hold the attention of a Texas Ranger for long. At least after speaking with Flint, Josie would have an end date to look forward to. Not that she particularly minded Heath—not him personally. Oh, he was nice enough and not bad to look at.

But he was a Texas Ranger. They sought out danger. That was their job. Even if he insisted on stopping by her ranch and doing chores in the morning, which it looked like was his plan, she couldn't get used to it…to him. Heath would leave soon and rush off somewhere that meant risking his life. It was best not to get attached to him in any way, even simply as a friend.

Really, it would be better if she got rid of the overly helpful man. At least in her personal life.

After changing into fresh clothes, braiding her hair and straightening the kitchen, Josie made her way outside and entered the barn. She found Heath sitting on a stool, hunched over the water troughs, scrubbing them out with all his might.

He glanced her way. "Animals are fed. Bedding's changed. I spotted a few fence posts that could use reinforcing."

How did he know how to take care of a ranch? It wasn't like a Texas Ranger had a lot of free time on his hands to care for animals and land and everything that went along with ranching.

"You don't need to do that." She paused in the doorway. "Actually, you don't need to be doing any of this." She crossed her arms. "Why are you here?"

"I thought I could help."

She propped her shoulder against the doorjamb. "I don't need any help."

Straw dust danced between them in the morning rays of light bleeding into the barn. Heath's eyes met hers across the space and he held her gaze. Raised his eyebrows.

Josie shook her head and walked forward. "I don't need *your* help."

"What if I said I was hoping to get more breakfast out of the deal?"

Even though he said it with a straight face, Josie was smart. She knew the man was trying to save her pride. Allow her to hang on to the idea that he was working for a good meal instead of pitching in because she was a lonely, pregnant woman. He could get a huge breakfast at the inn every morning if he wished and he was choosing not to.

Fine, then. She'd play along. Because that was better than admitting the truth.

"Oh. I see how it is." Josie clucked her tongue. "You're like some homeless dog. I made the mistake of feeding you and now you'll just keep on coming back?"

He dragged the first trough back to its corresponding enclosure. "Something like that."

Josie spun around and called over her shoulder, "Wipe your boots before coming into my house."

"Will do."

She went back inside and muttered to herself as she set the griddle on. She leaned her hip into the counter and braced her hand along her side. It was a blessing not to have to do all the chores this morning. Over the past week, her lower back had been hurting more often than not.

When the griddle was warm enough for a pat of butter to sizzle its way across the surface, she mixed the liquids and soaked six large pieces of fluffy bread. French toast and bacon. She'd make him some food, explain to him that he couldn't just show up here and take care of all her chores every day—even though she really did appreciate it—and then she'd ask him to leave again. No getting attached. Easy peasy.

Heath entered as she was filling cups with orange juice.

"All set." She gestured to the plate.

"Looks great. Smells even better." He nodded. "Let me just wash my hands."

Once he was back at the table, he said grace for them again and they both dug into their food. This morning Josie was glad to be heading into her third trimester—no more morning sickness. Food was her friend again.

"I didn't get to mending the fence posts today. But I will by the end of this week."

Josie's curiosity was piqued. She had to find out how he knew so much about ranching. "To be a Ranger, you'd have had to have worked for the state for a long time before then, right?"

"Eight years in investigations with the state before you're even allowed to fill out an application."

"So your entire adult life has been dedicated to police work?" He sounded a lot like Dale. Living…breathing the job.

His head bobbed. "I served as a soldier right out of high school and then went straight into the force."

"Did you ever see action?"

He looked down at his plate. "A tour in Iraq."

"Was it scary?"

Heath shrugged. "To be honest, I didn't have a lot going for me at the time and I wasn't afraid to die. I know that sounds bad." He moved his cup in a slow circle so the orange juice swirled around and around. "My father had passed away a few years before that, and my mom remarried pretty quickly. I'm afraid to say my stepdad and I butted heads from the get-go. More than anything, I joined the service to escape."

Heath wasn't afraid to die? She wanted to ask him about that statement, but she didn't really have a right to. Policemen and soldiers were alike in that way, weren't they? They always knew that not coming home was a possibility. But that didn't mean they weren't afraid of the possibility. Did Heath enjoy an adrenaline rush? Or was it something else?

Josie laced her fingers together and looked down at her palms. She didn't need to know because she wasn't getting involved with him. Not even as friends. He'd be around for a month and then be gone.

*Ask him something else. Anything else.*

"Did you grow up on a ranch?"

"No, a quiet patch of suburbia." He stretched out his legs under the table. "My dad was in law enforcement."

"Ah." Josie nodded. A lot of families were like that… Being on the force seemed to run in the blood. She cradled her belly. *Not you, little one! I won't allow it.* "Well, when did you learn all this stuff?" She motioned over her shoulder, in the direction of her barn. "How to take care of cows and pigs and fix fences? Last I checked they don't teach that on the force or in the army."

"They sure don't." He chuckled and set his napkin on the table. "My uncle Blaine has a ranch not far from here, near Waco. I moved in with him when things went south with my stepdad. Blaine put me right to work." Heath rubbed his hand over his smile. "He says there's no such thing as hands that aren't working on a ranch."

"Good for your uncle."

"I'm glad he did." Heath steepled his fingers. "If he hadn't done that, I wouldn't be any help to you now."

"What are you doing in Haven anyway?" Josie asked between bites. "Besides bugging me at my ranch, that is. And the calves mystery." She rolled her eyes. Not because she wasn't still scared about the possibility of a stranger having been hiding in the barn with her, but because it still seemed silly that a Texas Ranger was working the case. "We both know you didn't take a month off to investigate *that*."

Heath finished a piece of bacon. "Visiting Flint, mostly. And checking out the boys ranch, of course."

"Do you know someone who might need to go there?"

"Having resources for troubled youth stored up here—" he tapped his forehead "—is good in my line of work." He rested his forearms on the table. "How about you? Why do you volunteer there?"

Josie shrugged. "Everyone in Haven pitches in."

"Did your husband?"

Not at all. Dale always gave the place a wide berth. "Why do you care—"

"I'm sorry." He held up a hand. "Forget I asked."

Josie plowed on anyway. "I'm a member of the Lone Star Cowboy League. We support the boys ranch. I'm there because I want to be, but also because it's my duty as a member of the League. My husband wasn't a member. You have to be a rancher to be involved… Dale wasn't one. I only just joined. After." She looked down.

"You didn't have to answer," Heath said. "My question was out of line. Job hazard. I'm used to asking whatever I want to know." He smoothed his hand down his jaw. "How about this… Who's your favorite kid on the ranch?"

She shifted her cup around and around in her hands. "I don't have a favorite."

"Of course you do." His voice was gentle. "Who is it?"

"I guess, if I absolutely had to pick… I'd probably say Diego. He's had a hard road in life. He's this bright little guy who always has a serious expression on his face. Like he's working out a math puzzle at all times." Josie pulled a face, imitating Diego. Heath answered with a soft grin.

"His hair is almost black and his eyes are dark and soulful." Josie found she was smiling but couldn't help it. "He and I get along really well because he loves the cattle. He's always the first one at the barn waiting for me and wants to pitch in on anything having to do with the calves. You could say I have a soft spot for him."

Heath leaned forward. "What's Diego in for?"

"In for?"

"All the boys there, they're troublemakers. They wouldn't be sent to the ranch if they weren't. What's Diego's issue? What'd he do wrong?"

Josie bristled. There was nothing wrong with Diego. Nothing at all. Sometimes a child needed special attention. Sometimes they needed a change from normal life in order to work through something. But living at the ranch certainly wasn't a punishment.

"You still don't think well of them. Even after our talk yesterday?"

Heath's expression became unreadable. "I know good, well-adjusted kids don't end up there. Normal kids are at their homes…with their parents. I know bad things have happened at the boys ranch in the past."

"With that attitude, it's a wonder you're willing to help Flint solve his case at all." She scooted out of her seat and collected both of their plates.

"Attitude?" Heath turned in his chair so he could continue facing her as she moved to the sink. "That's not attitude. It's the truth."

Josie dropped the dishes into the sink with a loud clang and turned around. "Those boys are flesh and blood with feelings and dreams and they just want to be loved and accepted. Same as you and me." She laid her hand along her collarbone. "If you can't see that, Officer, then you aren't that great of a detective after all."

"I'm sorry." He looked down, studied the table. "Perhaps you're right. After everything, I guess it's hard to see them any other way."

"After everything? What's that supposed to mean?"

"My dad was a Texas Ranger. I don't think I told you that before. But he was."

He'd said his dad worked in law enforcement…but they were both Rangers? That was amazing. "You followed in his footsteps?"

Heath nodded. "I wanted to honor his sacrifice." He looked down at his hands as if the lines on his palms were the most interesting things in the world. "Fifteen years ago, my father was working a case at your boys ranch."

Josie's heart sunk. She sucked in a loud breath. As someone who'd lost a loved one to the thin blue line, she knew where his story was going.

"They found him dead. Three bullets. Near the main barn on the old property."

"Oh, Heath." Josie crossed the kitchen and laid a hand on his shoulder. She squeezed. "I'm so sorry." She blinked against the burn of tears, his words dragging up the ache of her loss.

"My dad's murder is still a cold case. Unsolved."

His hand came up and covered hers. It was warm and comforting. Josie's throat spasmed. She missed the friendly touches of her past life…a quick hug, a shoulder brushing against a shoulder, holding a hand. She missed it so much she ached.

She drew her shaky hand out from under his. "Now that you mention it, I remember hearing about it on the news when it happened. It was a big deal in a town like Haven."

He swiveled in the chair in order to make eye contact. "I'd like to solve the case, if I could."

"That's why you're here, isn't it?"

"Among other reasons." He shrugged. "But I'd like to keep that private as much as I can, if you don't mind."

"Of course." She nodded. "My husband was a deputy." Josie dropped into the seat beside Heath. Close enough that their knees bumped. "It started as a routine traffic stop and turned into him never coming home." She got the words out before her throat clamped up again. But her voice pitched higher at the end, betraying her.

Heath reached over and took her hand. He held it between both of his. For a minute they sat in silence. Allowing each other to deal with their loss. Finding comfort in the fact that someone else understood.

Finally, Heath cleared his throat. "I'm sorry you had to go through that. No one should have to lose a loved one that way."

She dabbed at her eyes and nodded. Staying in the pain, reliving everything, wouldn't help her or her child. If Heath was still hanging on to the pain of losing his father, he needed to move toward letting that go, as well. But Josie knew how hard that could be. Still, she racked her brain for a way to encourage him.

She squeezed his fingers. "I know you said you would yesterday, but this is one more reason why you should volunteer at the ranch. There are ranch hands still working there who would have been working fifteen years ago. Someone might know something, Heath. Don't you see?"

Heath looked off to the side for a second. Josie had noticed he did that when he was considering something.

"Some of the ranch hands are still there?" He captured her gaze again. His dark eyes swirled with questions. "Are you sure about that?"

"Very sure. I'll have to talk to some of the old-timers, but I think I can get you a list of the names of people who still live in town who worked or volunteered when it happened."

Heath rose to his feet. "Get your shoes on, Josie. Let's head to the ranch."

One hand on the steering wheel, the other cocked on the open window, Heath maneuvered his truck toward the boys ranch.

He stole a glance at Josie.

She'd wriggled more personal information out of him in the past two days than he'd told his coworkers in the nine years he'd worked for the Texas Department of Public Safety. They were the branch of the government that the Rangers functioned under. In order to be considered for the position of Ranger, Heath had worked as a state trooper for eight years first, in their investigative unit. Still, he was one of the youngest guys to be made a Ranger in a long time. He had a hunch that those in upper management remembered his father and that had paved his way. After all this time, he should be used to keeping a tight rein on his personal life, but Josie had somehow slipped under his defenses.

The woman should consider going into detective work.

She caught him looking at her and hugged her stomach. "My truck *is* just fine, you know. I could have driven myself."

They'd gone toe-to-toe over her truck. She'd called him overbearing and he'd insisted on having the vehicle checked out before she continued to drive it. Texan winters weren't bad, but still, anything could happen.

And that thing wouldn't be able to handle another accident if she did get caught in bad weather at some point. She'd said that was what caused the last fender bender, a storm. It was raining and she missed the stop sign. Ended up broadsided by a sedan.

Heath's stomach tightened. The idea of Josie and her baby in an accident didn't sit well with him. Not one bit.

He forced his fingers to relax his grip on the wheel. "Like I said before, let me take a look at it tomorrow. I know a little about cars."

"You know a little about everything, don't you?"

He popped his gaze back to her for a second, fighting a grin. This woman had exercised his smile muscles more than he cared to admit. "I've picked up things here and there."

"I don't like it." She looked out the window.

"Let's make sure it's sound before your baby comes," he added softly.

That did her in. She sighed and ran a hand across her stomach. "I guess that makes sense. If you're sure you don't mind."

He threw on his blinker to turn into the ranch. "Have you had someone install a car seat for you yet?"

She laughed. "I still have three months."

"They usually suggest doing it before…before it's too close to your time. Just in case. Babies have a way of appearing whenever they want to."

"And how do you know so much about babies?" She poked him in the arm a few times as she talked. The way his little sister used to when she was trying to be annoying. Although, when Josie did it, the action felt endearing.

"Not babies." *Those* he knew nothing about and

never would. "Car seats. I was trained as a car-seat technician when I worked with the troopers. I could teach you how to install one, if you'd like."

"I'll think about it."

Josie had the door open and jumped down to the ground the second he put his truck in Park. She had told him on the way over that she needed to meet up with the minister who volunteered at the ranch. She'd catch him later or maybe find a ride home with someone else. He'd make sure he found her before she wanted to go home. Because her place was on the way back to the inn where he was staying… That was the only reason he should drive her home, of course.

Heath shook his head. She *was* trying to shake him. Poor woman. Did she really understand what he did for a living? Once he made his mind up about something, he could be pretty stubborn. The trait came in handy in his profession.

Still…what must she think of him for showing up at her house two days in a row? He'd do it tomorrow, too. And the day after that. The woman was alone and pregnant; she shouldn't be managing the ranch on her own. Besides, she was the eyewitness to a possible crime. If the wrongdoer had spotted her, then Josie could be in danger. He wouldn't scare her with that notion, but he'd stick close until things were sorted out.

Heath spotted Flint straightaway. He was near the heavy machinery, but when he saw Heath's truck, Flint came striding across the yard. A big black dog yapped circles around his feet.

Heath grabbed his white Stetson, pushed it onto his head, then tucked his badge into his back pocket as he stepped down from his truck. He took in the barn, the fence posts, the large home—it was impossible for Heath to turn off his investigative eye. His brain seemed programmed to constantly log information, and look for weaknesses or issues. Things to fix, help, protect.

The black Lab bounded toward Heath, its tail smacking his legs while it used the running board on Heath's truck to jump up into the driver's seat, which put the animal at head level to lodge a full lick attack on Heath's neck and face. Heath groaned and good-naturedly shoved the dog's nose away so he couldn't lick him any longer.

"Cowboy, down." Flint reached around Heath, grabbed the dog's collar and tugged him out of the truck. "Sorry about that." Flint finally looked at Heath. The two men were about the same height, but that was where their similarities ended. Where Heath's eyes were dark, Flint's were blue; same for the hair—Heath had black to Flint's blond.

"He's only two," Flint apologized. "Still learning his manners."

"It's fine." Heath used the sleeve of his white button-down to sop the worst of the drool from his neck. "He still has better manners than most of the people I deal with." He adjusted his hat. All the Rangers wore them for work, but he'd gotten so used to the feel of it on his head, Heath usually wore the Stetson at all times.

"Got a minute?" Flint released the dog and it took off toward the barn where a group of school-age boys were working a few ponies in the arena. Flint set his hands on the edge of his belt.

"Right. Down to business."

Flint laughed.

Neither of them was a chitchat type of guy. That

was probably why they'd gotten along so well during basic training.

"I've been meaning to ask you about something," Flint said as Heath came over.

Heath propped his hand on the edge of his holster. "I have all the time in the world right now."

Flint leaned against the giant wheel of a tractor. "I told you about the gentleman who died and left us this new property. Didn't I?"

"Cyrus Culpepper."

"That's the one." Flint shook his head. "I forgot about how good you are at remembering things—facts."

"That's what they pay me for."

"Well, I got some more facts for you, then." Flint hooked his thumb in his pocket. "Culpepper left terms in his will. You know how our ranch used to be located on the other end of town?"

Heath nodded. The boys ranch had moved into their current location—the land from Culpepper's will— only a week ago. Before then, they'd been located on a smaller piece of land.

"Well, it turns out Culpepper was one of the original residents from when the boys ranch was first started. One of his stipulations for us to keep the property and everything else he left is to have the original boys from the ranch back for the anniversary party in March."

Heath waited for the punch line. There was always a punch line.

Flint shifted his weight, obviously uncomfortable with whatever he had to say. "I was tasked with tracking down a man by the name of Edmund Grayson. Maybe it's a long shot, but I was wondering if you might be related to him. Does that name sound familiar?"

*Edmund Grayson?* But it couldn't be…could it?

Heath sucked in a rattled breath.

Of course he knew that name—but no, it wasn't possible. He wouldn't believe it. Heath straightened his spine. Kicked his boot against one of the tractor tires to shake free of the dirt.

He cupped his hand along his jaw. "That's my grandfather's name, but he was never a resident at any of these ranches."

"Is he from the Waco area?"

"He is that." Heath nodded. "Born and lived in this area most of his life. He was a state trooper until he retired and moved to Florida."

"Edmund's not a common name," Flint said gently.

It wasn't, but there had to be two of them. If his grandfather had lived at the boys ranch, Heath would know. Wouldn't he? That was something his father or grandfather would have mentioned at some point.

"I'm telling you, you have the wrong guy. My grandfather never went to one of these ranches. I'd know if he did. He would have told me. Especially after what happened to my dad, that would have come out at some point."

Flint shuffled his feet. "It's imperative that all four of the original residents are found and reunited at the celebration in March. If that doesn't happen…we'll lose all of this." He raised his hands to encompass the land. "Edmund Grayson is a unique enough name. I haven't been able to find another one with ties to the Waco area."

"It's not my grandfather."

"Ask him. What's it going to cost you to ask?"

An olive branch and then some.

Heath hadn't spoken to the man in years. He'd received a congratulations card in the mail when he'd been appointed a Ranger, but that had been their last contact. Maybe he'd ask Nell, see what she thought before poking at the old bear.

"Please?"

Heath sighed. First investigating the incidents at the ranch and now possibly reaching out to his estranged grandfather. Flint was sure getting a lot of favors out of him this visit.

He gave Flint one stiff nod. "I'm not promising anything, but I'll see what I can find out."

# Chapter Four

Josie shooed Heath away when he tried to help her down from his truck. One would think he'd have caught on by now that she liked to get down from the cab on her own.

They'd been following the same routine for a week now. Every day he showed up at her house just after sunrise. He did all the chores and then polished off whatever food she placed in front of him, praising her cooking the entire time. Then he drove her to the ranch, and while she worked her volunteer shift, he poked around and talked to people about possible leads for the incidents that had occurred there. She'd given him a list of names of ranch hands to talk to who would have worked at the ranch when his father was murdered and she'd noticed him engaging each of those people in conversations, as well. The boys ranch was blessed to have so many people who either volunteered or continued working there faithfully for so many years.

After talking with Flint, a few days ago Heath had started leading an after-school club for boys interested ·· learning how cops investigate crimes. They called their little club *detection class*. A majority of the older boys had instantly jumped at the chance to spend time with a Texas Ranger. Josie couldn't blame them; Heath was good company.

On her way toward the office, Josie spotted a few of the boys in the pen with the calves, trying to put a lead line on one of them. As she drew nearer, she recognized Riley, one of the oldest teen residents at the ranch, and his ever-present shadow, ten-year-old Morgan, as they moved to corner the skittish dairy calf everyone called Honey. She was a favorite among the kids because she had a marking that looked like a heart on her forehead.

Morgan was a shy kid who was sometimes easily discouraged. If Honey kicked one of the boys, Morgan would probably not want to be around any of the calves any longer.

Josie stepped into the pen and secured the door again. "Careful, now. She scares easily." Josie held up her hands. "Shh, Honey. It's okay, girl."

"Be careful, Ms. Markham." Riley's eyes went right to Josie's pregnant belly. "How about you let me get up close to Honey instead? If she kicks, I'll be fine." At seventeen, the boy towered over Josie.

Right. She'd forgotten how protective the older boys were about her. There was no way Riley was going to let her get close to Honey until he had her tethered.

As small framed as she was, Josie's pregnancy had showed almost immediately. Once the older boys noticed, they'd taken it upon themselves to try to ease her load. They were always offering to carry things for her or go in with the bigger animals when needed or pitch in when her truck got a flat the other week.

All their gestures were sweet, but sometimes the

extra attention grated on her all the same. The whispers of Dale's repeated instructions to her—*don't do this, you can't handle that, no I won't let you have a farm, my wife won't smell like cattle if I have anything to say about it*—were never far behind whenever she let one of the boys help her.

She had to remind herself the boys' intention wasn't to control her—they weren't trying to tell her she wasn't capable of doing those things. They were showing they cared about her.

Josie stayed and encouraged Morgan as he led Honey around the pen a few times. She headed toward the office housed at the ranch once the boys left the pen on their way to their next lesson. The director had left a message for her earlier in the day. Bea, the director, had said she wanted to speak with her about how long Josie planned on volunteering…*considering her condition.*

Josie held her head high as she strode past the blond receptionist, Katie Ellis, who was talking animatedly on the phone to someone about an electric bill. On a normal day, Josie would have stopped to say hi to Katie because the two women were good friends, but Josie didn't want to interrupt Katie's conversation. Instead she gave a little wave and the receptionist rolled her eyes and pointed at the phone. Josie stifled a laugh.

Josie went over again what she had decided to tell Bea. She wanted to volunteer as long as she was able, although the pains in her back told her that it might not be too much longer. But she still had three months until her due date. Plenty of women worked right up until they went into labor; surely Josie could help around the ranch until then.

*Be brave. Be strong. Speak what's on your mind.*

The director's office was empty.

Josie swiveled back toward Katie, who was just hanging up the phone.

"Bea's not in?"

Katie sprang from her seat and came over to Josie, offering a quick hug. "You seriously just missed her. She had to run into town." Katie motioned for Josie to follow her to the front of the office near a set of wide windows, her bouncy hair swishing as she walked. "She shouldn't be long. Do you want me to have her find you?"

Josie pressed her shoulder into the wall for support. "Heath has to leave early to run some errands today. I leave when he leaves, so I might not be here when she gets back. And I'll be late tomorrow because I have a doctor's appointment."

It had been a week of Heath stopping at her ranch in the morning, helping with chores and then sharing breakfast. He'd discovered some problems with her truck and declared it unsafe to drive for the time being. Something about her radiator and, even more concerning, he explained that the main rail for the frame of the vehicle had been weakened by the accident and needed to be replaced. He'd told her to call her insurance agent and have the truck junked, but Josie couldn't do that. Not yet. She simply needed to have the rail fixed…and figure out how she'd pay for that. Surely that would be less expensive than buying a whole new car. She'd been a housewife for ten years and all of their bills and credit had been in Dale's name. No one would give her a loan. She had to build up credit before she could buy a new car.

Katie's green eyes danced with mischief. "Well done

there, with Heath. You snagged a good one. He's a looker."

Josie rolled her eyes. Katie was young and single and had her radar set to locate and catalog all single, attractive men. Josie knew for a fact that there were at least three ranch hands who were suffering from crushes on Katie, but Katie didn't seem to have eyes for them.

"I snagged nothing. Nor do I want to." Josie hooked her hand on her purse strap. "*Snagging* isn't in my repertoire any longer."

Katie gave her a deadpan look. The younger woman was hopelessly determined to see everything through romance-tinted glasses.

Josie let out an exasperated breath. "Heath has a strong protective streak. Most guys in his line of work do. The man saw a pathetic pregnant woman all on her own and turned keeping an eye on me into a mission. That's how these types of men function. Everything's a mission." Josie popped her hands onto her hips. "Mark my words, come end of November, he'll be gone on a new one and will have long forgotten us here."

"You're hardly pathetic." Katie's eyes grew wide. "You know that, right? You're one of the strongest people I've ever met."

"Thank you for saying that," Josie whispered. She didn't feel very brave. She was fighting tooth and nail to survive and hang on to her dream at the same time. Was that brave? Or was it foolish? Could the two be the same thing?

"I mean it."

Josie glanced out the window and her gaze landed on Heath. He was near the doors of the learning center, a small building behind the main house that held a library and had tables for the boys to do their homework on. A group of boys surrounded him.

Katie nudged her elbow. "You like him." *Nudge. Nudge. Nudge.* "Admit it."

Josie turned away from the window, but only slightly. She still wanted to keep an eye on…outside. She sighed. "He's a pest. That's what he is."

"The kids already adore him. That didn't take long." Katie jutted her chin toward where one of the young boys hung on Heath's arm as he talked to an older boy. "They were all raving after his first lesson in…what are they calling it? Investigation? No. It was…*detection*." Her voice took on a dramatic flair. "That night the boys put together this large-scale spy game that went all over the house. Whenever an argument broke out, they'd end it with 'Tomorrow we'll ask Heath. Heath will know. Heath knows everything.'" She laughed.

Thinking about the impact that Heath was already having on the boys in only the few days he'd spent on the ranch, Josie felt her lips tugging into a smile. "He does seem to have a way with them. I've been volunteering at the ranch for five months and haven't been able to connect with the boys the way he has in less than a week."

"Well, I mean, he does have an unfair advantage." Katie tapped the pocket on her pink shirt. "Shiny badge."

"And I'm a pregnant lady." Josie laid her hand over her abdomen. "That counts against me for coolness points."

"No way. The boys are so excited about your baby."

That was true. The boys were always asking what

they could do or if they could be invited to the baby shower.

Josie tapped the glass, pointing at Heath. "Still not as cool as a Texas Ranger."

"True. Very true. But then again, none of us measure up to that. We can't. Not in a boy's mind." Katie crossed her arms and leaned against the edge of the window. "So are you going to fess up that something's going on between you two or not?"

"We hardly know each other and he leaves in a few weeks." Josie walked away from the window. Enough staring. It wasn't kind to her heart to watch him so much. "For good."

"His company's out of Waco. That's not exactly far, Josie."

"Sure, Waco's not that far away. But he said he doesn't live in Waco proper. A distance outside of that. And it doesn't matter whatsoever if he lives five minutes away or ten hours away because the second his vacation is over, we'll be out of his mind. As we should be."

"You two have already talked about how far away he lives?" Katie smiled excitedly. "Oh, this is promising."

He lived forty-five minutes away…too far for her to want to think about keeping up a friendship while trying to juggle her ranch and the baby who would be arriving soon.

"He's a Texas Ranger." Josie's voice went up a little, just a little. Why didn't anyone understand what a big deal that was? "Do you know what kind of cases they work? The sort of danger they're in?" Josie hugged her stomach. "After what happened to Dale…" Her voice broke.

Katie's eyes went soft and she placed her hand on Josie's arm, offering a squeeze.

Josie swallowed hard. "I don't want any connections to law enforcement. Not ever again. I don't want to care…even a little bit…for someone who could be killed as part of their job."

"Couldn't that happen to any of us, though?" Katie said softly. "Not just a lawman. But…I could get in a crash on the way to work. One of the ranch hands could get thrown from a horse and land wrong. Someone could be stampeded."

"That's not the same." Josie shrugged away from her touch. "It's not the same as willingly knowing that part of your job requires you to have a gun pointed at you at any time of any day. Freak accidents are very different than dealing with criminals."

"But doesn't that say something, I don't know, something really great about a man's character when he's willing to do that?" Katie started to pace. "That he's willing to stand in the gap between society—people they don't even know—and the dangerous stuff? I mean, in a way it's a lot like how Jesus stands between us and the worst possible fate. It's very Christlike, being ready to lay down your life for someone."

Josie adjusted the strap on her purse and inched toward the door. "And there. You just made my point for me. They killed Jesus."

Katie's face fell. "That's not at all what my point was."

She had to get Katie off the topic or else they'd go around in circles. Josie wasn't going to change her mind. "Moving on…"

"Okay, but please admit that he's cute. You can do

that at least, right?" Katie pointed over her shoulder out the window. "He's got that tall, dark and handsome thing working for him. Not to mention he has that *I'm here to rescue you* vibe, as well."

She was trying to make right for having upset Josie. That was Katie's way. She was kind, a peacemaker. Josie sighed. She would ease Katie's conscience by making light of everything. "He is handsome. I'll agree with you there." That was part of what made him so dangerous.

"He's here until the end of the month?"

Josie nodded.

"Are you bringing him to the Thanksgiving celebration?"

"I didn't think to ask him."

"Please do." Katie's phone started to ring and she headed back to her desk. "I need a head count, and the boys who are sticking around for the holiday will want him there. They already look up to him so much. They'll all try to sit at his table."

"I'll ask him."

Her hand hovered over the phone receiver. "As your date?"

Josie walked backward through the doorway. "Absolutely not."

Katie shrugged. "Hey, you can't blame a girl for trying. I wish someone would get Pastor Walsh to ask me, but it's like he doesn't even notice I'm here." She sighed and then picked up the phone, answering it in her cheery voice.

Everyone at the ranch knew that Katie had her heart set on the young pastor. Too bad Andrew Walsh was just about clueless when it came to women. He was a great preacher, but started to fumble and grew shy whenever the younger women in the congregation tried to speak with him. Pastor Walsh volunteered at the boys ranch, often holding lessons with the boys under the large tree in view of the office window near where Katie sat.

Josie laughed as she walked down the hall, making the connection for the first time.

Maybe Pastor Walsh wasn't so clueless after all.

Heath slowly paced in front of the row of boys. They were all at attention, soldier straight as their eyes followed him. He'd led them into the barn—the "crime scene"—so they could start collecting clues.

"Now, I've roped off the area so that our evidence won't be disturbed. Take some time to study the scene and then we'll talk about what we see."

The boys inched forward, craning their necks.

Heath had locked them out and set up the crime scene. Shoe impressions on the dirt ground, areas where the suspect would have stumbled under the weight of what they stole and a clear area where the item was stolen from. Those three things should be enough to tell them who'd committed their make-believe crime.

If only his other investigations—the real ones—would go as smoothly. He'd started to move down the list of people Josie had given him, people who had worked at the ranch when his dad was murdered. Talks with the first four on the list had only produced people who said they were sorry for his loss and knew nothing. Heath scrubbed his hand over his jaw. She'd given him the contact information for a few people who still lived in the area but no longer worked at the boys ranch. Those were his next leads. His only leads.

So far there was no news on the mischief at the ranch, either. Everyone claimed they hadn't seen or heard anything suspicious, although a few people suggested a man by the name of Fletcher Snowden Phillips as a suspect. Supposedly he had a grudge against the boys ranch. Heath would look into that next.

But first, his detection class.

Heath shook away his thoughts so he could give the boys all his attention. "So what do you see?"

A boy with a mop of brown hair raised his hand. "Footsteps." He pointed.

"Good eyes." Heath nodded. He crossed to where he'd set up a pail and then motioned the boys over. He'd made sure to wet the dirt earlier, until it was muddy, and sank the borrowed shoes in deep so they'd leave solid places to cast impressions. "I need two very detail-oriented helpers."

All hands shot up. He pointed to an older and younger boy, probably sixteen and ten respectively, and jerked his head for them to come closer. Heath hadn't learned all the boys' names yet, but he meant to. Whenever he got a name right, they beamed like they'd just won a prize.

"We always try to collect as much evidence as we can, but we have to balance that with being as careful on scene as possible." He squatted near the pail, all eyes following him. "In this profession, we live by the motto 'Do Right the First Time' because we don't get second chances. Not with a crime scene, and often not when questioning people."

"Do right the first time," Stephen, one of the older boys, muttered. Heath had made certain to learn which one was Stephen right away because the teen was on his list of suspects for the string of incidents that had occurred at the boys ranch. "That seems like a tall order. Almost impossible."

A female voice cleared her throat near the doorway. *Josie.* Her auburn hair cascaded over her shoulders and the sun shone behind her, lighting her petite frame.

Heath's throat went dry. He couldn't take his eyes off her.

"That's a good point, Stephen." Josie stepped into the barn and joined the boys. "It's really difficult to do right the first time. At least, in life it sure is. I know I usually mess up before doing something right. I don't know about all of you, but I'm really thankful that Jesus has grace on us when it comes to our lives."

She draped her arms around two of the shorter boys' shoulders. "But that's not what Heath is talking about. He's talking about using your God-given gifts and talents to bring glory to God. By Heath doing his best to get everything right and not miss a thing when he first arrives at a crime scene, that's a form of worship for Heath. He's honoring God. See, God cares about justice. God cares about what Heath does…about what you guys do in your lives, too. I hope y'all understand that."

A couple of the boys nudged each other and looked back and forth between Heath and Josie, but Heath couldn't pay too much attention to what that meant yet. Josie's words thundered through him. Was she right? While he had been raised in the church, Heath had intentionally distanced himself from God after his father's murder. What else could he do? As a young man, he'd pleaded with God to bring about justice for his father and it never came.

Because God didn't care. Not about his family. Not about him.

But deep down, Heath had decided that he could *make* God care. If he caught enough wrongdoers, if he solved enough cold cases, if he served enough victims… perhaps then God would care about him, perhaps God would answer his prayers.

A foolish notion, but he'd held on to it for so long.

Was it possible, like Josie said, that his police work— the normal tasks he did every day—brought glory and honor to God? If so, it made all the late nights and striving worth it. Maybe he wasn't as far from God as he thought he was.

It was something to think about.

The kids were staring. Waiting for him to say something.

Heath found his voice. "When we find deep shoe prints, we always try to make a cast of it as quickly as possible." He explained how they used a mixing powder called dental stone. "It's the same stuff the dentist uses to make impressions of your mouth." He eyeballed the amount of powder and then had his two helpers measure water into the pail. "Looks great." Heath rose to his feet. "Stir it until it looks like pancake batter. It'll take about five minutes. Take turns. Believe me, that's a long time to stir something."

He handed talcum powder to another student. "Dust this into the shoe prints. Go ahead and do all of them and we'll pick the best one to cast."

When the dental stone was ready, he helped them pour the plaster-like substance into three of the best prints and then gave his helpers high fives. "Well done. We'll let those set until tomorrow and then we'll pull them up and try to find the shoes that match them. Normally I'd photograph it all first, and if these were muddy prints indoors on carpet or hard floors, the process would be a little different."

He was losing the younger ones. Too many details. He had to remind himself these weren't recruits. That was who he was used to training. Heath roped off the crime scene. "That's probably enough for today. You guys are dismissed. We'll start back here tomorrow and solve this crime."

Josie chatted with a couple of the boys, ruffling their hair and laughing with them, while Heath packed up his things.

Stephen found him a few minutes later. "I wanted to tell you that I really like your class. I'm learning a lot."

"Knowledge is great, son. But more important than learning something is using the information for good. Will you promise to do that, Stephen? Use this training for good?" Heath hooked his hands on his belt. "Someone who wanted to commit crimes could learn how police investigate in order to do things without getting caught."

Stephen's face fell. "You think I'd do that?"

"I didn't say that. Not at all. But you have a responsibility, everyone in our class does, to use what you've learned to help people."

"I plan to." Stephen nodded solemnly. "I wish… I mean, it would be so cool if I could be like—" He shook his head. "I look forward to whatever we're doing tomorrow." Stephen hurried away, almost as if he was embarrassed.

Josie wandered over to Heath. "They like you and I'm starting to think the feeling's mutual."

Heath could say the same thing about whatever was happening between him and Josie. He cared about her—that was undeniable. But what did that mean? He knew it was stronger than his normal desire to protect those when his station demanded it. With Josie, he *wanted* to protect her. If someone else offered to, he'd argue with them for the right.

He swallowed hard. "I'm still keeping my radar up around Stephen."

"He didn't do anything wrong."

"Then there's nothing to worry about."

Her face dropped. "Heath."

"Josie. You realize what I do for a living, correct? Sometimes the least likely person is the guilty one. Some people are good at hiding their real self. I've seen a lot of really bad…really messed-up stuff. Okay?" He hated bursting her bubble, but he'd seen too much in his life to think otherwise. "All of these boys here are capable of the worst sins imaginable. We all are. That's the hardest part in law enforcement. Crime isn't one size fits all. Have a little faith in me? In my process?"

"These boys are here to heal." She placed her hand on his arm. "Are you? That's the entire purpose of this place."

He pressed his teeth together—wanting to fight what she was implying but finding himself at a loss for words. He wanted answers about his father's death. He wanted to write *Case Closed* on the file. Would doing that heal him?

He sure hoped so.

# Chapter Five

Sunshine blazed through the wide front windows in the waiting room of Josie's doctor's office. She narrowed her eyes and adjusted how she was sitting, fighting nausea. Sometimes the oddest things—like bright light—could make her feel sick since becoming pregnant.

The receptionist at the front desk tapped away at her keyboard. It sounded unnaturally loud. A nurse in scrubs behind the front desk was taking a personal call, arguing with someone about how expensive her daughter's orthodontia was.

Josie ran her fingers over her forehead.

Heath rose from his seat beside her and crossed to the windows. He adjusted the blinds so the light didn't hit them in the face any longer and then came back to his seat. Josie's heart tightened at his ability to read a situation and take care of needs without asking questions. Heath Grayson was a man of action.

Too bad action often led to danger.

Josie swirled the sticky orange drink around and around in her cup. The nurse had explained that she had five minutes to down the highly sugared liquid and then they'd have to wait an hour. After the hour, the nurse would do a blood draw and they'd be free to go. A normal test for gestational diabetes, everyone assured her.

Even still, Josie couldn't help but worry. If the test came back positive... No, she couldn't think about that right now. She couldn't take one more disappointment this year or one more setback on her dream. All of Dale's life-insurance money had gone to paying off his debts, leaving her and their child with nothing to live on. If she was told to stop working, her ranch would go belly-up and she'd have no way to provide for her child. The only job Josie had ever worked was as a nanny while she and Dale dated, but he'd wanted her to stop after their wedding. And she wouldn't be able to take on a nanny position with a newborn in tow, now, would she?

She wrapped her free hand over her stomach.

*Lord? I know I don't have much to give in return. Less than much. I have nothing to offer You. Nothing at all other than a heart that wants to learn to trust You. I'm penniless and in need and I don't like being like this. But...please take care of us.*

Heath laid down the magazine he was flipping through. "Feeling any better?"

Josie swallowed another gulp of the horrible orange liquid. "Yes, thank you. The sunlight's intense today."

He chuckled and leaned back in his chair. "You could sure say that."

The air-conditioning kicked on, swirling the leaves of the potted tree in the corner of the office.

A nurse in maroon scrubs popped her head through the door near the reception area that led to the exam rooms. "Jenny Price?"

There were three other ladies in the waiting area. The one wearing purple, who looked like she might be past her due date or possibly carrying twins, slowly got to her feet and headed into the back area.

"Listen, Heath." Josie laid her fingertips on his forearm. "They said this'll take an hour. I'm sure you have better things to do. Thank you for the ride, but you don't have to wait here. I can call you when I'm done."

He traced a finger over the design on the side of his boot. "I don't mind waiting."

"It's an hour."

"I've sat patiently at stakeouts that lasted for ten. No worries."

She should know by now how stubborn this man was. Besides, it was nice to have company in the waiting room, even when they weren't talking. Simply knowing someone else was there with her was enough. She'd attended every other appointment alone. Not that Heath would come into the room for the blood draw or to listen to the heartbeat. She wasn't about to let that happen. But still…he was here and he didn't have to be.

Josie forced down the rest of the drink and then brought the cup to the front desk so they'd know to start her hour. She eased back into her seat and rubbed her palm back and forth over the fabric covering her thigh. "So, stakeouts? Those are dangerous, aren't they?"

Heath shrugged. "Only if they spot you before you spot them. Which doesn't happen often. Not being seen…that's the nature of a good stakeout after all."

Sure, but every stakeout carried the possibility of being seen. Being ambushed. Being murdered. "Do you have to do them much?"

He nodded. "More now as a Ranger than I did when I was a trooper."

Josie sighed and moved to lean away from him. She needed the few inches of distance she could get in the chair. It was far too easy to start depending on Heath. Come December she'd miss him, miss the breakfasts they shared as they discussed ways to improve her ranch, miss the sweet way he equipped the boys and made them feel capable, miss how he read her mind when she needed something and seemed all too willing to put her first.

Pain radiated underneath her collarbone. She pressed her fingers into the spot. Heartburn. Probably just heartburn. That happened these days.

Heath angled toward her. "Did your husband— Dale, right?"

She nodded.

"Was he an investigator? Or…?"

She allowed a moment before answering to take a few deep breaths while the pain in her chest subsided. "A sheriff's deputy. On their truck-enforcement division."

His eyes went to her stomach and then came back to meet her gaze. "I said it before, but I'm real, real sorry for your loss."

They fell into silence. Heath flipped through a magazine about birds and Josie had to bite her tongue because she wanted to ask him if he was a nature-lover. Did he enjoy camping? Hunting? There was so much about Heath she wanted to know, but she swallowed down the questions. Knowing him would make her care more.

Still…the quiet felt too heavy. Perhaps it was the glucose drink she'd just put into her body, sending her heart into overdrive, but she couldn't sit without fidgeting and wanted to talk.

Josie cleared her throat. "The boys ranch has a huge Thanksgiving dinner buffet that a lot of the families come out and attend. Most of the boys and the staff will be there."

Heath set down the magazine and rested his elbows on his knees. "I know about the Thanksgiving celebration."

"Oh, that's great. So will you come?" *With me?* "Katie—she works in the front office—asked me if I knew if you were going to attend. She needs a head count."

"I…ah." Heath pressed his hands together and touched the sides of his pointer fingers to his lips, deep in thought. His gazed was fixed on a carpet stain shaped like a running dog. "Thanksgiving…" He sat up slowly. "I don't know. Thanksgiving's not a good time for me."

Her heart sped up and her gut tightened. Or maybe the baby kicked? "Are you planning to leave before then?" Why did her voice have to go up like that?

He shook his head and pulled his phone from his pocket. "I'm here until the end of the month." He got up. "Will you excuse me?" He started backing toward the door. "I'm late returning a call."

Josie watched him walk out of the lobby and stand outside the front doors. She'd scared him off by inviting him to the Thanksgiving meal.

"He wants nothing to do with the boys ranch," she mumbled to herself. How had she forgotten that? A week with the boys hadn't changed his opinion. Not if Heath couldn't even stand the thought of sharing a holiday meal with them.

With her.

Josie fanned at the burn in her eyes.

"Dumb hormones." She blinked away her tears.

It would be silly to cry over Heath, a passer-through who had made it perfectly clear that he didn't respect the boys ranch and, come the end of November, had no intention of staying involved in anyone's life beyond his friendship with Flint.

What did she even want from the poor man? For him to attend the Thanksgiving dinner and decide he wanted to move to Haven and keep doing her chores and driving her around for the rest of his life?

Even if—it was outlandish to entertain the thought—he developed feelings for Josie beyond friendship, she wanted nothing to do with a lawman. So picturing a friendship lasting past November was foolishness on her part and she only had herself to blame for these emotions, because Heath had been up front with her from the get-go.

No more letting her hopes get out of hand.

It was in the low fifties outside. Heath felt ten times better with the sun on his face, away from the freezing-cold office. He knew medical offices were purposely kept cold to discourage germs from multiplying, but running the air-conditioning in November felt like a stretch.

Things had gone topsy-turvy in the past week. He wanted to keep the boys from the ranch at a distance, but then again, each one of them made him smile in their own unique ways. So far he'd found them to be good kids, respectful and hardworking. But that didn't fit with the image in his head. Fifteen years ago they'd found his father bleeding out near the barn after he'd taken on an assignment to protect one of the residents. Heath had always secretly assumed the youth turned on him.

Still believed that was the case.

He let out a long sigh. Trying to solve his father's case was foolish. Every night, he'd gone over the paperwork in the files, looking for a clue the investigators might have missed, but he found nothing new. Nothing besides plummeting hope. But that wasn't new, either.

Beyond all that, confusion reined in his thoughts for another reason. Heath had long ago decided he would never marry. Never get involved with a woman because he wasn't about to leave a family in the same position his father had. Heath couldn't do that. It was easier to care about no one than to start to care and realize the best thing for them would be for him to fade from their life.

He was playing with fire when it came to his friendship with Josie Markham. Hopefully, neither of them would walk away at the end of the month burned. Then again, it might be too late for that where he was concerned.

Advice. That was what he needed. A voice of reason.

Heath leaned against the brick building, pressed the button for his saved contacts and pulled up the first number. Nell.

She answered on the second ring. "Long time, no hear, big bro."

"Sorry about that. The last few months have been busy." Heath pushed away from the building and paced the length of the parking lot.

"Last few months?" She laughed. "Don't kid yourself. You're always too busy." Her voice was warm, kidding, but her words hit a soft place in his heart. They stung with truth.

He bunched up his free hand and glanced back through the front doors at Josie. So small and fragile and yet brave despite it all. So alone.

His throat went dry. "Nell? I'm sorry—all those years ago when Bill left— Would you forgive me for not being there for you?"

"Where is this coming from?"

"Just thinking." He ran his hand over his hair. "I wished I'd been there for you."

"It wasn't your responsibility."

He hooked his free hand on his belt. "Doing something out of love is more important than out of responsibility, don't you think?"

"Don't beat yourself up about it. You were stationed out of Lubbock at the time. That's a five-hour drive, Heath."

For Heath's entire career, he'd thought himself selfless—spending his time helping victims, seeing that justice was served—but in reality, he'd been selfish. He'd used his positions as soldier, trooper, investigator, Ranger... all of them to feel like he mattered. To convince himself that he was a good person. All the while, not investing in the people who actually knew him, like Nell and his mother. Never going out of his way for them.

When was the last time he'd called his mom?

He paced down the parking lot again, his boots clicking over the pavement. "I should have taken a leave from work. I had the time. But it never even crossed my mind to do that. It was selfish of me not to. I see that now."

"Heath. Seriously. Stop. I'm fine. Carly's fine. There's nothing to forgive."

"I could have been there." He kicked a rock into the abandoned yard in between the medical office and a small strip mall.

"But you weren't. And know what? I'm over it. I moved on. I'm with Danny now and I have this hunch he's going to propose around Christmas and you'd better be there for the wedding."

His feet stilled. Nell married? Danny was a good guy. Heath felt a smile tug at his lips. "I wouldn't miss it."

"You promise?"

"Yes. And I love you." He ran the toe of his boot over a patch of tar covering a crack in the road. "I don't really ever say that, do I?"

"Not ever." Her voice hitched a little. "I love you, too. And I definitely like this warm and fuzzy version of you, but I have to ask, where is this change coming from?"

"The anniversary of Dad's death is coming up." November 22 would mark fifteen years.

"Two weeks from now." Her voice sobered. "Is that… Are you okay?"

"I'm in Haven for the month. Investigating it."

"Are you sure that's a good idea? You had such a hard time when…well, you know."

"I was fifteen. Dad was my hero."

"Not was. He is. Dad's still your hero. Mine, too."

"I want closure." Nell would argue that they had closure at the funeral, like she always did, so Heath pressed on, "More than what we have."

"So investigating Dad's death has led to you thinking about the past?"

"Not just that. There's this lady here." Heath cupped his free hand around the back of his neck. "Josie. She's in a situation like yours except her husband was a policeman. He lost his life in the line of duty."

"Oh, Heath. You have a soft spot for her, don't you?"

He debated denying it, but Nell knew him too well for that. "You could say that."

"Have you told her?"

"Her husband of ten years died six months ago." He spoke slowly so his sister would understand how impossible the situation was. "No. I haven't told her that I care about her. It wouldn't be appropriate and I don't think the attention would be welcome." Josie often brushed away Heath's offer to help her out of his truck and fought him when he tried to lighten her load. The mix of being standoffish yet sweet was messing with his head.

"But you care about her?" Nell squealed. "This is huge. I haven't heard you talk about a girl since high school."

"I've been busy."

She clucked her tongue. "Not anymore, though. Not this new and improved Heath Grayson." There was a smirk in her voice.

"How'd you do it…all alone, with Carly?"

"I just did, because I had to. But it was hard. I wouldn't choose to walk pregnancy and birth and caring for a child alone if I had to. I thank God every day for Danny strolling into my life last year. He's already such a help." Carly was singing along to something loud and high-pitched in the background. Nell and Heath both shared a laugh over it. "Heath…you could be Danny in Josie's life. You realize that, don't you?"

He wanted to argue with his sister, but that would just lead their conversation in a circle, so he didn't. "She invited me to the Thanksgiving dinner at the boys ranch."

"Tell me you're going."

He started to head back toward the doctor's office. "Since Dad, well, you know. Thanksgiving's never been my thing."

"So change that. Go. I want you to go."

"There's something else I want your opinion on."

"Shoot, Ranger."

Leave it to Nell.

He chuckled. "Flint's trying to locate all the original boys from when the ranch opened. They're looking for someone by the name of Edmund Grayson… They think it might be Grandpa."

She gasped. "No. It can't be, can it? He would have said something. We'd know, wouldn't we?"

"That's what I thought, but should I call him? Make sure?"

"I wouldn't. He's such a grumpy old man. I'd be afraid to ask because he might get offended. You know how he can get."

Of course he knew; that was why Heath hadn't made the call yet.

He noticed Josie fidgeting inside, so he tied up the conversation with Nell with a promise that he'd be around to celebrate Christmas with them and he couldn't wait to see how much Carly had grown. He also found out what Carly's favorite shows were so he'd have a better shot at picking a gift she'd enjoy. From now on he would be more involved in his niece's life. Next year, he wouldn't have to ask Nell for suggestions because he'd know what Carly wanted.

At least, that was a goal to aim for.

When he went back inside the waiting room, he smiled at Josie and they sat together without talking while they listened for her name to be called. Heath liked that. Just sitting near her, knowing she was safe.

How would he ever go back to his old life next month? The life where he was just as alone as Josie had been, but hadn't ever realized how lonely he really was? His five-hundred-square-foot apartment would feel like a solitary prison after this.

After the doctor's appointment, Josie walked beside Heath on the way back to his pickup truck. Because of construction taking place in the parking lot, they'd had to park in the strip mall next door.

"I can go get the truck," Heath offered again.

"Walking is good for me." She charged ahead and shooed away the offer of his arm, although it would have helped to lean on him as they picked their way across the yard spanning the distance. But she'd decided to put space between them.

As they entered the strip-mall area, the door to the first store flew open—the nail salon—and a lady with brass-blond hair and French-manicured fingers cut in front of them. She wore skintight jeans and a shirt bearing a bedazzled cowboy hat and the words *Everyone Loves a Texas Girl*. Josie would know those sparkly high-heeled sandals anywhere.

Avery Culpepper.

Despite her decision moments ago to not touch Heath, Josie grabbed his arm and gently tugged so he'd slow down. "That's Cyrus Culpepper's granddaughter," Josie whispered. "She came after the reading of the will. A real troublemaker."

Heath bobbed his head slightly. "I've seen her a few times at the Blue Bonnet Inn. She made a ruckus over wanting poached eggs the other morning." Heath eyed the woman as they got closer. "Culpepper? The man who left his property to the boys ranch?"

"The same."

Avery had her smartphone in her hand as she tottered toward her aging red convertible. "I can't wait until I can shut down that ranch. Turn out all those bratty little children and sell the place for some real cash. I have so many plans for that money. You have no idea."

Josie dug her fingertips into Heath's arm. He wrapped his hand over hers and offered a sympathetic look.

"Of course I think I'll win!" Avery smacked away at her gum. "Ain't it my right?" Her car chirped when she hit the unlock button. "What claim do those snivelers have to it? I've got the name. They've got sad stories." She dropped into her driver's seat and adjusted the rear-view mirror. "Sad stories don't win lawsuits and I aim to sue." Avery peeled out of the parking spot, veered around an elderly woman pushing a shopping cart out of the grocery store and tore down Main Street.

Heath worked his jaw back and forth as he held the passenger door open for Josie. She climbed in and waited for him to slowly round the front of the truck and enter on the driver's side.

But not a moment longer.

"She can't take the ranch away, can she?"

Heath shoved the keys into the ignition, but then let

them dangle. He leaned back in the seat and took in a long breath. "I don't know. I hope not."

"But you know laws."

"I know crime codes. Not inheritance laws."

"The will named the Lone Star Cowboy League for the property, not her. She can't do this to those boys." Josie swiped at tears.

"Shh." Heath's face twisted when he saw she was crying. He reached over and squeezed her hand. "Don't cry. Please don't cry. I'll talk to Flint. I'll help however I can."

"Why? You don't even care about the boys ranch." She shot the words at him because she was frustrated and needed an outlet for the emotions that threatened to drown her. They had never affected her like that before pregnancy.

Heath kept his voice soft, calm, as if he was speaking to one of her orphaned calves. "Just because I don't trust every single person there, doesn't mean I want the place shut down. The work being done at the boys ranch is valuable. I'll tell Flint what we heard and—"

"No. Gabe." More tears. "He's the president of our chapter of the Lone Star Cowboy League. We have to tell Gabe."

"All right, we'll tell Gabe. Hey. Everything will be okay." He squeezed her hand again before letting go. "We'll fight for this place if we have to."

Not trusting her voice, she sucked in a rattling breath and nodded.

Heath wrapped his arm over the steering wheel and turned on the engine. He backed out of the parking lot and headed in the direction of the boys ranch. "I'm sorry about how I acted earlier, when you asked me about Thanksgiving."

She gripped the armrest, just to have something to hold. "I shouldn't have assumed you'd want to attend."

"It's not that. It's only…my father was murdered a few days before Thanksgiving. At the boys ranch—at the old location. So, this is all a mess for me right now. If that makes any sense."

"Oh, I didn't know." She placed a hand on his shoulder, not knowing how else to comfort him. "That makes complete sense. Why didn't you say something?"

"I'm saying something now."

Josie shook her head. Men.

Heath turned down the music and glanced her way. "What I'm trying to say is, I'd be happy to come to the Thanksgiving dinner, that is, as long as you promise to sit at my table." His smile lit up every angle of his face.

She wanted to say she'd sit beside him at every meal for the rest of their lives if he was willing.

*Careful, heart.*

*Act like it's no big deal. Because it's not.*

Josie removed her hand and rolled her eyes at him. "Are you sure there will be room? My guess is all the boys will be fighting to sit at your table."

"I'll save a seat." He winked at her. "Right beside me."

Josie swallowed hard. "Then, sure, I'll sit at your table."

And she'd probably regret it once December started… but she'd do it for the sake of the boys at the ranch. They'd be ecstatic once they learned Heath would be there.

Okay, maybe it wasn't just for the sake of the boys,

but she wouldn't give hope wings by dwelling on the feelings stirring in her heart. Because truth be told, if that hope sprung wings, the only ending for it would be a crash landing.

## Chapter Six

Neither of Heath's real-life investigations were going so well.

Despite talking to several staff members who had worked at the boys ranch while his father was there and going over the case files every night back in his hotel room, he wasn't any closer to figuring out what had led to the murder.

Could a resident at the ranch really have committed the crime and then been able to cover it up? Unfortunately, he'd encountered crazier scenarios during his course of duty. Heath's gut twisted. It was impossible to imagine one of the boys who currently lived at the ranch engaging in such an act. The very thought made him feel ill.

Then again, there had been different boys there fifteen years ago. Who knew what they'd been like? Other than his father. And Heath could hardly ask him.

When it came to the recent happenings at the boys ranch—a missing therapy horse last month, some minor thefts and the person Josie had witnessed setting the calves loose—he didn't have much to go off of there, either. Although, his hunch was still that one of the boys had a penchant for pranks—nothing sinister. So far, there hadn't been any more incidents while he'd been volunteering. Heath guessed—if someone local *had* been committing crimes—his presence was enough to keep wrongdoers away. Haven was a small town. Everyone knew a Texas Ranger was loitering around the boys ranch by now.

They'd wait until the guard dog went home to strike again.

*So don't leave.*

He sighed and scrubbed his hand over his jaw.

At least the made-up investigation his detection class was working on was going better.

Since a few new boys had joined the boys ranch in the past week, Heath had put off going back to the fake crime scene. He wanted to give the new boys a chance to catch up before bringing the group to solve the case. But today he'd led them back to the makeshift crime scene in the calf barn. They'd pulled up the shoe imprints and were passing them around for inspection.

Most of the boys were staring at him, waiting. Had he been silent so long?

He cleared his throat. "So what else do you notice about the crime scene?"

Heath passed in front of the row of students. He paused in front of Joey and Damon, two of the new boys to arrive at the ranch that month. Joey's red hair stuck out at odd angles, making it look like he'd just woken up in spite of the fact that it was already midday, but he'd been smart as a whip during his talk about interviewing suspects. Damon was smaller, shier. His deep brown eyes matched his skin tone.

"Damon, notice anything?"

Damon squinted and tilted his head. "Maybe the person was shuffling?"

"Great eye." Heath stepped across the yellow crime-scene tape and squatted near the shoe prints. "Damon's correct. Does everyone see how some of the prints are dragged together and spaced closer?" He pointed so they could see exactly what he was talking about. "These little details are real important when it comes to identifying the suspect. It's also the sort of thing that'll help you win a case in court."

Stephen raised his hand. Heath still needed to find a time to speak with the young man about the calves getting loose. He made a note to do that before he and Josie left for the day.

"Yes, Stephen?"

The teen stood at the back of the pack and rose up a little, probably on his tiptoes, to gesture toward the back wall. "It looks like the shoes went deeper into the mud way over by the wall there."

"Excellent." Heath rose to his feet. "Any ideas as to what would cause that?"

Joey licked his lips. "The ground could have been muddier there. Wetter?"

Heath nodded. "That's definitely a possibility. However, the ground slopes toward the drain in the center of the building, so it's unlikely that moisture would pool near the walls. But I really like the way you're thinking. The deeper impressions mean something…"

Stephen crossed his arms, narrowed his eyes and tilted his head a fraction. "The person was carrying something heavier when they stepped there."

Heath winked at him, letting the teen know he was correct. "Which raises the question…what's missing?"

Riley, one of the older boys, looped his arm over a shorter boy Heath had noticed was always his shadow. "I got this one. I asked Josie. She said the old hand-crank ice-cream maker used to be on that ledge there." He gestured toward the back wall near the footprints. "And now she can't find it."

"Sought out and interviewed a victim." Heath whistled. "I'm impressed. You just might be a future Ranger." He grinned at the boys, surprised by how much fun he was having teaching them. "So here's what we have so far." He used his fingers to tick off the clues. "A stolen ice-cream maker, someone who might have shuffled and the knowledge that the ice-cream machine might have been a struggle for them to carry."

"And this." Stephen wiggled the plaster cast of the shoe impression. "The print doesn't have any logos on it, and most of the bottoms of tennis shoes have that. Right?" He looked off to the left. "So I think it's someone who doesn't wear shoes like that. But most everyone else around here wears cowboy boots, and it doesn't look like that, either. It's too wide…almost like a loafer or something."

Joey laughed. "It looks like an old-lady shoe."

They were so close to cracking the case. Heath almost gave in and told them, but he bit his tongue. They'd piece it together soon enough and the ranch cook, Marnie Binder, had a surprise waiting for them when they did.

Stephen's eyebrows rose. "You know, now that you said that…it looks like Marnie's shoes! She makes sense with the ice-cream maker, too." He took off running out of the barn and banked a hard left toward the big house. Heath motioned for the rest of the boys to follow. Moving as a pack, they sprinted past the learning center and barged into the back of the big house, where all the boys lived.

Marnie was waiting for them in the kitchen, a huge smile plastered across her face.

"You're the thief!"

"It was you!"

"Give the ice-cream maker back!"

The younger ones were jumping up and down, excitement pulsing around the room.

Marnie threw back her head and laughed as she raised her hands in the air. "You caught me, all right." She grinned back at Heath. "I see you've got a whole brood of junior detectives on your hands."

"My future boss is somewhere in this crowd. The next generation of Rangers, right here." He spanned his hands to include all the boys. Each one looked so proud of himself, proud and confident. Heath's chest swelled, although he couldn't brush away the pang of sadness he felt, too. He would have benefited from a father figure to encourage him after his dad passed away.

Nell had said he could be someone like that for Josie. But what about for these boys? Was it possible God had placed Heath here for a reason far beyond his father's case?

He shook away his thoughts.

Heath had a job to do. An important one. As a Texas Ranger, he had one mission, one goal—to uphold the law. That duty put him at risk daily. Attachments slowed an officer down...made him go soft when difficult, snap decisions needed to be made.

"Well, now." Marnie popped her hands onto her hips. "Looks like I got a bunch of junior Rangers here who can help me whip up some ice cream."

The boys clapped and whooped and took turns scrubbing their hands in the sink, the older boys monitoring the progress of the younger ones. Marnie pulled the ice-cream maker out of hiding and sent a few of the boys to gather the ingredients from the fridge, where she'd set them to chill.

"You." She pointed at Heath. "Rock salt. Back porch."

"Yes, ma'am." He tipped his hat and then fetched the heavy bag from the rack on the porch.

Marnie lined the boys up and had them take turns churning the hand crank. "You, too, Ranger." She motioned Heath forward. "Only those who crank get to eat it."

"Then by all means." Heath rolled up his sleeves and worked the crank for a few minutes. It took more strength to do than he'd figured, but the boys cheered him on. After his turn, he backed away from the group in order to observe everyone.

When was the last time he'd spent an afternoon smiling this much?

Months? No...years had passed.

He worked his jaw back and forth, trying to piece together the puzzle of his own life. Somewhere along the way, Heath had stopped experiencing joy. Perhaps it was because in his profession, he saw more of the bad side of humanity. He'd been a firsthand witness to so many horrible situations because of the cases he investigated, he'd forgotten how to or even felt guilty if he enjoyed life.

Experiencing joy shouldn't make him feel guilty,

though. If memory served him right, the Bible said something about joy being a by-product of someone knowing God. Somehow he'd forgotten that along the way.

Who knew how long the joy would last? Nothing in life was guaranteed. But for now, he'd savor it. Store it up so he had enough to last him all the lonely years for the rest of his life once he left the ranch and Josie.

Josie reached for the next pile of T-shirts to fold.

Part of her role as mother's helper was to assist and sometimes take over the day-to-day tasks that needed to be accomplished in order to keep the house at the boys ranch running. All the boys had household chores, but they also had responsibilities outside of the house. Josie was there to help fill in the gap.

For as long as she could during her pregnancy.

"Didn't we just do laundry the other day?" She laughed as she tapped the top of the leaning tower of folded shirts. "How do these boys manage to go through so many outfits?"

The three housemothers who were folding alongside her all shook their heads and smiled good-naturedly. Dark-haired Laura was on her right; the woman was kindly and served as a sort of grandmother figure in the house. Abby giggled on Josie's left. She was Josie's age and full of life. The two had become fast friends when Josie started volunteering. Across the folding table stood Eleanor, who wore her red hair pulled back in a low ponytail.

Eleanor sighed. "Just wait until your little one arrives. You'll be amazed how someone so tiny can make so many messes. When my first came, I remember doing a load of laundry every day and not being able to understand where all the towels and blankets were coming from."

"Here, Josie." Laura pressed a basket full of clean kitchen rags and towels into her hands. "Go ahead and bring these to Marnie and then you can head to the barn." She nudged her with a grin. "We all know you didn't get to take a peek at your calves yet today."

"What are you going to do when those calves all grow up?" Abby joked.

Josie felt a smile bloom on her face. "Get new ones. Believe me, ladies, there are always orphaned calves to be had." She did a little bow and then propped the basket on her hip as she headed down the hall. Although she loved catching up with the housemothers, Josie really did miss the calves whenever she didn't get to see them, and because of her doctor's appointment that morning, she hadn't made her way to the barn yet.

She maneuvered out of the way as the door to the office opened and revealed Gabe Everett, president of their chapter of the Lone Star Cowboy League and liaison to the boys ranch. His broad shoulders ate up all the room between the doorjamb.

"Just the man I needed to see." Josie wedged the laundry basket against the wall because it was getting heavy.

Gabe's blue eyes cut her way. He was a powerful figure in town—a single, wealthy rancher who was more handsome than any cowboy had a right to be. Josie always found herself intimidated around him, but she forced her lips to move anyway.

"Will you be around awhile longer?"

"I can be if you need me." Gabe hooked his hand on the top of the doorway.

"Okay, let me just find Heath and we'll be right back."

Thankfully, the man in question wasn't difficult to locate. Josie turned the corner and found Heath with a bowl of melting ice cream in hand, surrounded by a bunch of chatting boys.

Diego sprang to his feet and rushed toward her. "Ms. Josie!" He bounced beside her and she couldn't hold back her laugh. She'd admitted to Heath when she first met him that Diego was probably her favorite. He'd won a special place in her heart because of their shared interest in cattle, his infectious smile and his cheerful spirit to match. Sure, the boy had baggage—the years before he came to live at the ranch had been difficult ones—but he was growing every day. Josie had a connection with Diego that none of the other adults working at the ranch seemed to have obtained. Her friendship with the boy was one of the things that had confirmed for her that all the extra volunteer hours were what God wanted. Not only that, the time had blessed her, too.

"Want to taste the ice cream?" He thrust a bowl under her nose. "We made it ourselves. Heath let us after we solved the crime."

"Looks delicious, but maybe later."

Diego's eyes went wide. "See how many of us there are?" He solemnly shook his head. "There won't be any later."

While Diego was talking, Heath set down his bowl, got to his feet and crossed the kitchen to her side.

"Here. Allow me." He eased the basket from Josie's hands and passed it over to the counter near where Marnie was leaning. "You might want to take them up on the ice-cream offer. It's the best I've ever had."

"Homemade is the only way to go," she agreed but still passed. She'd overdone it on the burritos at lunch. But they'd been delicious and she was pregnant. So there.

Heath rested his hands on his stomach and nodded. "The only thing that would make it better would be a side of pumpkin pie."

Josie chuckled. "Is that your favorite?"

"It is. And I've yet to partake in any yet this fall."

Diego's gaze shot back and forth between them like he was watching a tennis match.

She really shouldn't kid with Heath so openly in front of the boys, but she was having too much fun to stop. "We'll have to rectify that."

Diego wedged himself closer to them. "Do you know how to make pumpkin pie?"

"I have a secret recipe and everything." She tapped the tip of the boy's nose. He gave her an impulsive hug and then dived back toward the table for seconds.

Josie scanned the room, happy to see Heath engaging with so many of the residents. Her gaze landed on the tiniest boy in the room, a small blond boy. Tucked between Riley and Stephen, Flint Rowling's little boy, Logan, shoveled spoonful after spoonful of dessert into his mouth. Logan was only six, younger than most of the boys in Heath's class. He and his father lived on the property, but Josie knew Logan was supposed to be with either Flint or his nanny. Neither person was in the room.

She stepped closer to Heath. "Does Flint know Logan's here?"

Heath rested his hand on the right side of his belt. Josie noticed he did that a lot. Probably a reflex of carrying a gun there his entire career. He was used to something being there to set his hand on.

"His son?"

She inched so she was right beside Heath and the boys couldn't hear. "The little one. Over there."

Heath frowned. "I didn't notice him before. Is he not supposed to be in here?"

"Not unless his nanny is with him." She held out her hand. "Give me your phone." Heath quirked an eyebrow, but handed over his phone. "Thanks. I forgot mine at home today." She swiped at the screen. Heath's screen had a plain, boring solid color background and a couple of icons. She found Flint in his recent calls, just like she'd guessed. She pressed the green button.

Flint answered right away.

"Hey, it's Josie."

"Heath all right?"

"Yeah, I stole his phone. I just wanted to make sure you knew Logan was up at the big house."

"He's *what*?" Flint's voice rose.

Josie turned away from the group. "He's okay." She kept her voice soft in an effort to calm Flint down. "He's in the kitchen here eating ice cream."

"I can't believe this." Something clanked in the background. Had Flint thrown something? "That child will be the death of me."

Josie turned a little, immediately seeking out Heath's gaze for comfort. Why was Flint getting so worked up over Logan being at the big house? "I only wanted you to know where he was. He's not causing any trouble. That's not why I called."

"He'd best not be misbehaving. He's in plenty of trouble for wandering off again as it is."

"He's only a kid," she pleaded. "I'm sure he simply enjoys spending time with the others. No harm done."

"Oh, harm's done, all right. Disobeying's not okay. Not on my watch. I'll be there soon." He hung up. From his tone, she expected him to come barreling through the door any second.

What was going on between the boy and Flint? Every interaction she'd seen between them in the past had been positive, but Flint had sounded really upset. Logan was only six. Surely Flint knew that a six-year-old boy would try to get up to the ranch to hang out with the other kids every chance he could.

*Calm down.* Flint was on his way and he was Logan's father. It wasn't up to her to judge. Perhaps Flint was having an off day. Even still, she silently prayed for God to soften Flint's heart toward his son and give him compassion and the imagination to remember how it was to be so young.

She reached out to touch Heath's arm. "When you're done, I need you. Gabe's here and I want you to come with me to tell him what we heard."

Heath wiped his hands off on one of the clean towels. "I'm done now." He dumped his bowl into the wide kitchen sink and instructed the boys to wash up. "Marnie's taking the watch from here."

Relieved of his duties, he followed her back to the office and Katie pointed them toward a small room where Gabe waited. Josie made introductions and then launched into the details about seeing Avery Culpepper earlier in the day.

"She said she's planning to sue for all of the property and then she's going to kick the boys out. Can she do that?" Josie wrung her hands over and over again as she talked.

Heath reached across and laid his hand on top of hers. A silent message to relax, take a breath. He was there to fight beside her.

Gabe leaned back in his chair. "Unfortunately, Avery has bite behind her threats. She met with our leadership last week and tried to cut a deal. We give her one hundred thousand dollars and she'll sign something that forfeits her ability to sue for the land, but if we refuse to pay, she says she'll hire a lawyer and battle us in court for everything."

Josie gasped. Tears pricked in her eyes. "I can't understand how someone could be so coldhearted toward this organization."

Gabe rested his hands on the desk. "I hear she's been telling anyone in town who will listen that Cyrus did her wrong."

Heath nodded. "I've heard her griping some back at the inn. I never realized it had to do with Culpepper or the ranch, though. She didn't say any names. Only that she's been treated poorly by her family and they'd pay for it."

Gabe scrubbed his hand over his jaw and exhaled loudly. "Not only did he deprive her of a relationship with him, but he left her only that run-down cabin where he was raised. And we all know the old property isn't worth much."

It was better than the ranch Josie was scraping out at her father's old fishing cabin.

Josie balled up her hands. "We make out of this life what we put into it. Some of us fall on hardships or get a bad road of it, but that's no one's fault. That's life. We can't wait for or expect handouts to make it all better."

Gabe's eyes softened with understanding. "I know that, Josie. Believe me, I do."

Heath's spine straightened. "Don't give in to her threats. It's not lawful, her trying to manipulate the League that way."

Gabe frowned. "No disrespect, Ranger, but I'm not so sure it's that easy. Avery has a proper claim to the land if we can't meet *every* stipulation in the will. If we don't find *all* the original men for the reunion, we can't keep the ranch anyway."

Josie ran her fingers over the worn fabric of her jeans. She swallowed hard. "Is there... Would there ever be a situation where the League would pay her?"

"I can't say what we'll do if we end up with our backs against the wall. If we're forced to..." He shook his head. "All I know right now is we stand no chance unless the anniversary celebration is a success. That has to be our focus."

Josie leaned forward. "We'll find the men. We have to."

Gabe tilted his head, glancing Heath's way. "Flint mentioned you might be related to Edmund Grayson. Has anything come of that?"

Heath stared down at the toes of his boots. "Nothing yet. But I'm planning to call him."

Gabe tapped the desk. "It's imperative that all four original residents of the boys ranch are reunited at the ranch in March." His words were slow, deliberate. "If we don't meet the demands of Cyrus's will, we'll lose the property."

"I understand." Heath hooked his ankle onto his knee

and rested his hand on top of his boot. "I'll check with him."

"Soon?" Gabe urged.

"You have my word."

Josie turned to face Heath, but he wouldn't meet her gaze. Why hadn't he told her he might be related to one of the original boys? What was he hiding?

## Chapter Seven

Heath probably shouldn't have left the ranch right after their talk with Gabe, but he'd needed air. Space. Time to think. Still, he shouldn't have walked out of there without letting Josie know his plans.

Gravel churned under the tires of his truck as he steered it back up the long drive to the boys ranch. He hadn't been gone long, but the daylight hours were growing shorter. The sun's last tips of light blazed orange over the far field, but it would dip away to darkness soon.

If he wasn't on vacation right now, if he was home—as much as his tiny, sparse apartment could be called that—the streetlights would give a sense that there was still time to accomplish something more that day. Out in the country areas like Haven, the sun dictated the work hours. When it went down, it was time to relax.

But Heath couldn't relax just yet.

"You left her. You just…left." He worked his jaw back and forth as he popped the truck into Park. Everyone who lived on the ranch would be inside of the large house by now. Josie among them, no doubt. By this time, dinner was long over.

His phone vibrated in his truck's console. Maybe it was Josie. She'd spotted his truck and was headed out to join him. Wishful thinking. She'd mentioned earlier that she'd forgotten her cell at home today.

He grabbed his phone and glanced at the screen. Nell. He hit Accept.

"I figured I'd start calling and checking in on you," she said.

"I'm glad you did." He filled her in on everything that had happened since their last conversation, including his failed attempts at coming up with leads for the happenings at the boys ranch and their father's murder. Many interviews, but no possible suspects. He told her all about Josie, too.

"So you're just going to keep this girl—this Josie—at a distance?"

He pinched the bridge of his nose. "It's for her own good. I stay away from people because of my job. You know that."

"That's selfish, Heath. You've got to let people make their own decisions. If they want to love you and risk losing you, then that's their choice to make. Not yours. You hurt more than just yourself doing that."

"But, Nell, I could die. If… I… Like Dad. No." He braced his hand on his dashboard. "I chose to become a Ranger, and this is part of the price. I stay away from people to protect them. If I was around you and Carly all the time and then something happened, wouldn't it be harder?"

"Harder than going to your funeral and thinking, *He's gone and now I'll never get the chance to actu-*

*ally know him?* No, actually, it wouldn't. At least we would have known you fully. We'd have a storeroom of happy memories to cling to. Instead of *Well, I never really knew him—I wish I had, but now there's no hope of that.* See the difference?"

He'd never considered that. It hurt losing his dad, but they'd been close. He missed him so much *because* he'd been such a present father. Heath swallowed hard. "Painfully so."

"Then stop being such a mule and do something about it. You know what? You go right on ahead and call Grandpa."

"You said not to."

"I changed my mind. You're going to become just like that grouch unless you make some drastic changes in your relationships. I love you, but you've really got to get over this stubborn self-isolation thing you've got going on."

Heath groaned, but Nell was right. "I love you, too." He promised to call her after he talked to their grandfather.

After hanging up, Heath scanned the buildings beyond the house and spotted Flint's outline near the horse corral. The two hadn't spent as much time together during Heath's vacation as he originally thought they would, and the month was half over already. Heath jammed on his Stetson and headed toward his friend.

"You seen Josie around?"

Flint's shoulders went rigid and he turned around slowly. "We've known each other a long time now, haven't we?"

Heath froze. Was Flint angry? Frustrated? Flint's tone sent off warning alarms in his mind.

Heath forced himself to relax. "That we have."

"How long?" Flint folded his arms over his chest and speared him with a hard look.

Huh. Heath had seen that look before. Ten years ago at boot camp to be exact. Determination mixed with an equal measure of indignation. But now that look was honed in on him. Was this about Logan eating ice cream with the boys? Heath hadn't even realized Flint's son was there.

*Just answer the man's question.* "Ten years, or thereabouts."

"Ten years seems long enough to know someone." Flint cocked his head. "To decide if someone's trustworthy."

Where was this coming from? The two men had watched each other's backs during boot camp, during their time in Iraq. Heath trusted Flint more than anyone else in the world. To think his friend didn't return that conviction...

Heath widened his stance. "You saying you don't trust me?"

Flint shook his head once. "That's not what I said at all. I'd trust you with my life. Have before."

"Then what *is* this about?"

"Josie."

Her name, the way Flint said it, felt like a punch to the gut. Heath's mouth went dry. Muscles in his legs and arms tensed, ready to spring into action. "What happened? Is she okay?"

"Don't know." Flint slid his thumbs into his pockets and rocked forward on his boots. "I think that's something I ought to be asking you."

Heath couldn't stand the idea of waiting for Flint to

get on with the conversation. Evidently he wanted to confront Heath on something. *So do it.*

Heath rolled his shoulders. "Go ahead and spit out whatever wants to be said so bad it's clawing its way out of you."

Flint lowered his voice and stepped closer. "What are your intentions where Josie Markham is concerned?"

"You sound like her father."

"Well, Josie's father is dead." Flint's stare remained hard. "In fact, she's got no blood family left. All she's has is us on the ranch and those in the League. While I might not be family, someone's got to watch out for her."

Heath stepped an inch closer. He and Flint might have fought as soldiers together, but Heath had gone toe-to-toe with the roughest folks in Texas for the past ten years while Flint had hidden away at the boys ranch. Hold up. It was wrong of him to think such a mean-hearted thing about his best friend. Acting on momentary indignation never served him well. Flint wasn't hiding at the ranch, he was devoting his life to something good. Something worthwhile. However, Heath wasn't about to let Flint attempt to intimidate or talk down to him.

"Funny, considering I'm the one watching out for her." Heath thumped his own chest. "That woman was struggling on her ranch and working herself to exhaustion and still would be if I wasn't doing the chores over there." He gestured off in the general direction of Josie's ranch across town. "You were all letting her and her unborn child drive around in that death trap of a vehicle before I insisted on picking her up every day. She's gone alone to every doctor's appointment. None of you have bothered to go and sit with her there." Heath took another step closer to his friend and dropped his voice low. "So don't talk to me about you being there for her if it's only going to be in word and not deed."

Flint's arms went slack beside him. "Maybe there's more we all could have been doing to pitch in for her. Plenty I didn't think about. She's stubborn and doesn't let anyone know when she needs help." He took a deep breath. "But that's beside the point."

Heath backed off, giving them both some breathing room. "I'm struggling to see what the point even is."

"Are you leaving at the end of the month?"

Heath took another step back. "If by leaving you mean going back to work, yes."

"Exactly." Flint grabbed a bucket off the ground, sending a puff of grain dust into the air, and started for the barn door, signaling the motion-detecting flood-lights to turn on.

Heath captured Flint's arm, jerking him to a stop. "Exactly, *what*? What's that supposed to mean?"

"It means that you're leaving and you need to re-member that."

"I'm a bad person if I go back to work? That makes no sense whatsoever." Even as he said it, Flint's words rang true and echoed Nell's. Of course Heath had to go back to work in December...but that had been an ex-cuse to keep people at a distance, too.

Flint made a *tsk* sound with his tongue and shook his head in a slow, sad way. "For a man who has spent his life unraveling crimes, you sure have a hard time reading people."

Heath's throat went dry. He knew what Flint was getting at... Josie. Was Heath setting them both up for heartache? But it wasn't like that. He was helping her because she was alone and he'd want someone to do the same for Nell. She was also the witness to a crime, be it a petty one that didn't seem to amount to much danger, but still…

He pinched the bridge of his nose. "Josie's my friend. That's it, Flint. She and I both know that."

"Tell yourself that if it helps you sleep better."

*Enough.* He didn't want to fight with his best friend. Not anymore.

Heath let go of Flint's arm. "Is she in the house? I'm supposed to drive her home."

"Josie's gone." Flint rested his hand on the door handle, his back to Heath. "Macy Swanson—the tall blonde who reads stories out loud to the boys in the learning center—she drove her home after Josie saw your truck was gone."

"I was going to come back."

Flint glanced back at Heath over his shoulder. "Josie looked upset."

No wonder Flint had launched into an argument with him.

An ache spread through Heath's chest. He shoved the heel of his hand against the center of his rib cage. "She did?"

Flint turned to prop his shoulder against the door-jamb. "I saw her crying."

If Heath was a man given to cursing, now would have been a time to use one, but he'd long ago given up that bad habit. Instead, he kicked at the ground.

After they had finished speaking with Gabe earlier, Heath had made an excuse to leave the ranch for the rest of the afternoon. All to avoid Josie—only for a few hours. He had taken a drive, got his head together before seeing her again, because he'd noticed the way she'd looked at him after Gabe mentioned Edmund Grayson.

Josie would ask.

Did she know how much her examination made him mentally squirm? He couldn't stop wondering what she was thinking. No one had ever had that effect on him before, but Josie was a singular woman. Sharp and quick to figure something out, bold enough to ask questions, yet empathetic and kind when the answers were difficult.

The problem was Heath didn't want to answer her questions. Not today. Not when he knew she'd ask about his grandfather. She would have prodded into why he hadn't called the man yet. Josie had a way of making Heath crack wide-open with information.

Heath blew out a long puff of air. "I didn't mean to hurt her."

"Since you've been my friend a long time, I'm going to level with you."

*It's about time.*

"If you have no intention of sticking around past November, then stay away from Josie. Plain and simple." The bucket swung beside him. "The woman lost her husband this year, she's pregnant, had to leave her home and her entire life has changed. She doesn't need another setback." Flint looked away, toward the ground. "Don't...don't lead her on."

"Flint. I wouldn't—"

"Don't make her hurt."

"That's not my plan." But then...what *was* his plan? Once he was back to living at his apartment, he couldn't stop at her ranch every morning to take care of her. He wouldn't get to kid with her over breakfast or encourage her while she shared her dreams about her ranch.

Flint's nostrils flared. His knuckles went white around the bucket's handle. "Listen. I know what it feels like to think you're in a relationship. Think the other person cares about you. And then have them disappear as if you're nothing more than dried dirt on their shoe."

Realization popped in Heath's mind. Of course Flint's thoughts would automatically go to Logan's mom and her betrayal. Her name was usually off-limits, but Heath saw no way around it.

"I'm not like Stacie. I wouldn't do that. Making someone think, hope, and then leave…" Heath shook his head as words failed him. He envisioned the end of the month, driving away and never seeing Josie again. His heart sank into the toes of his boots.

But, he'd visit. They'd stay friends. Wouldn't they?

"Abandoning someone." Flint nodded slowly. "It's the worst thing you can do to a person."

"I'm sorry." *For what Logan's mom's did to you.* Flint didn't want to hear that.

Flint blinked a few times, almost as if he was refocusing. "Don't be sorry. Be smart. You head back to your apartment and your career in two weeks and we'll all stay here. What you've done to help Josie would be great if you were sticking around, but now you've simply given her something to lose again. So let her be between now and then. That's the best thing you can do."

"But what if…" Heath couldn't meet his friend's eyes.

"What if, what?" Flint set the bucket down by the barn door so he could use his hands to talk. "I know you. Being a Ranger is your life. That's the most important thing and there isn't room for much else."

"But—"

"Oh, you may think you care about Josie now. She's pretty and nice and depending on you. Any man would like that. But once December hits, you'll get assigned a case and that'll become your priority. Promises to visit will lag into months of getting pushed back until finally it's summer and Josie hasn't heard from you in six months."

Heath tugged off his hat and then scrubbed his hand over his hair. "I'm not that bad."

"You are. You forget people the second you don't need them."

Everything came to a screeching halt. Was Flint mad at Heath for not being a more present friend? Come to think of it, Heath hadn't been there for Flint at all when Stacie left him. How many people had he failed without realizing it?

"I… Am I really like that?" Hadn't Nell accused him of the same thing? Letting too much time pass between contacting her and not staying engaged in her life? Did Heath have any friendships that he kept up with? Sadly…no. He partially blamed his police work. There was so much about his job he couldn't discuss outside of work. Heath had watched that put strains on a lot of the married Rangers' relationships.

But it wasn't all police related. Most of the blame fell squarely on his shoulders. Heath kept people at a distance—for their safety, of course. If he wasn't so connected to them, then if the worst happened, they wouldn't need to miss him or mourn him at some point.

None of his relationships would be like when Dad died. That had been his plan.

Nell had challenged him to let people choose if they were willing to take that risk. Heath didn't know if he was capable of doing that, though.

"You don't want to depend on others," Flint said. "I get it. I think it's what makes you so good at your job."

Heath shoved his hand against the barn and hung his head. "But it makes me a bad candidate for being a friend or anything more in someone's life."

"Bingo."

"Ouch." He ran his hand down his face.

"Well." Flint grabbed his shoulder and gave it a quick squeeze before letting go. "I'm still willing to be your friend."

Heath nodded and stepped away from the barn. "I'm sorry I wasn't there for you. During everything."

Flint shrugged. "It happens. I'm not losing sleep over it. Don't you, either."

His friend's words tumbled around in his head as Heath took the long way back to town. Driving often helped him straighten out his thoughts. What Flint said made sense. He should stay away from Josie, but Heath didn't know if he could. Even when she wasn't nearby, he wondered how she was and where at the ranch she was and pictured her smile.

Flint was right about Heath being a bad friend, too, and he wanted to change that. But how could he if he was supposed to pull away from Josie? Wouldn't that be making the same mistake again—the same behavior that had led to his hurting Nell and Flint?

What was he going to do?

The long drive didn't help at all.

\* \* \*

Heath ducked his head, hoping to avoid Gabe as the man strode purposefully toward the ranch house the next day. When he'd stopped off at Josie's house in the morning like he usually did, she was nowhere to be found, and she hadn't answered her phone, either. Heath had gone so far as to send a text message, not something he was given to doing seeing as he had very few people in his life to text with. Still no answer.

If something was wrong, if she was sick or had an emergency or there was something the matter with the baby, she would have called him. Of course she would have.

Still, Heath walked a little faster.

Despite Flint's warnings, Heath needed to find Josie and apologize for leaving her stranded yesterday. As long as he dodged Gabe, he could duck into the calf barn and catch a moment with her before she went into the big house to help with the housework for the day.

"A minute of your time, Ranger?"

Too late.

Gabe spotted him and motioned him forward.

"Of course." Heath trailed Gabe to a rough picnic table situated under one of the large trees by the ranch house. "What's on your mind?" Not that he needed to ask...

"Were you able to get ahold of your grandfather?"

No surprise there.

Heath exhaled and looked up to examine the way the branches on the tree wove into one another—like they existed to support each other and if some of them weren't there, the whole tree would start to die.

"Yesterday wasn't a good day for me to do that, but

I'll have an answer for you by the end of the week." Three days to work up the nerve to make the call. Less than a week until the anniversary of Dad's murder. Last night he'd crossed off the last name on Josie's list of people who had worked at the ranch fifteen years ago. All dead ends. No new answers...only more confusion.

"There's something more." Gabe leaned against the edge of the tabletop and crossed his arms. "I hear you have some reservations about the boys here."

Heath snapped his gaze back to Gabe. "Josie told you?"

"She didn't have to." Gabe's face remained unreadable. If he ever got tired of ranching, the man would make a top-rate investigator. "But word gets around in a tight-knit place like this."

"It appears so." Heath rubbed the back of his fingers under his chin, then straightened his spine. "Whatever you heard, know that I think you all are doing a great thing here for these boys."

Gabe adjusted his arms a little. He had the build of a man who might best Heath in a takedown if he was a criminal. Good thing Gabe was about as noble as a person could be. Honest and hardworking, the man ran one of the most successful ranches in the area and spent all his free time volunteering. Heath admired the man for everything he was doing to help others.

"You think the boys here are all bad news, though, don't you?"

"I guess you could say that." Heath tried to choose his words carefully. "Normal kids are home with their parents. You get sent to a place like this because you're having issues or are too much trouble for your family to handle. That's a fact, and I'm the type who works in facts."

"You're not wrong about what *starts* the process of them being here. However, I find it hard to believe that you still consider these boys capable of putting one of our therapy horses at risk, endangering Josie's beloved calves or stealing from the staff that they care about."

True. After spending almost two weeks getting to know the boys in his detection class, Heath found it impossible to suspect any of them. Even Stephen— especially Stephen.

But the training that came with so many years in law enforcement told him there was always a chance. "I believe anything—often the most unlikely—is possible. I have to."

"Do you think these boys will leave here and go back to their troublemaking ways? That they're destined to be bad eggs, or however you want to phrase it?"

"Not all, but some will."

"So lasting change isn't real? It's not something we can actually accomplish?"

Heath bit back a groan. He didn't want to get into this discussion with Gabe. Not when he wasn't sure what he believed anymore. "I know that bothers you to hear, but I'm a realist. I don't think a person can do what I do and see what I've seen and not be."

Gabe propped himself up so he was sitting on top of the table. His demeanor said he wasn't bothered at all by what Heath had said. Or he was very good at holding his emotions in check.

"I don't think you know, but when I was young I used to be a resident at this boys ranch."

"You?" Heath stumbled over the short word. Gabe

was capable and prosperous, the president of the area's Lone Star Cowboy League—and he'd been a troubled kid? The two facts didn't seem to fit, but Gabe had no reason to lie about such a thing.

"Me." Gabe nodded. "I turned out better for it, just like the current residents will."

"What years?" Heath licked his lips. "How long ago were you here?"

"Not—" Gabe scooped off his hat and tapped it on his leg "—when your father was murdered. That was a good seven years after I left. I know it was a long time ago, but I'm sorry for your loss. It's why you came here, isn't it?"

"Originally, yes."

Gabe studied him for a moment before saying, "But not now?"

"I'm just on vacation." Heath held his hands up in a stop motion.

"Watch out, Ranger." Gabe hopped down from the table. "You might find you don't want to leave. This place has a way of healing people." He stopped beside Heath.

"Funny." Heath shook his head. "Josie said the same thing."

Gabe pointed at him. "Smart lady, that Josie." Then he headed toward the ranch house.

And Heath went to search out the woman he'd spent half the night awake thinking about.

# Chapter Eight

The sweet smell of banana bread flooded Josie's senses. She swallowed. Hungry. Wasn't that always the case these days?

Then again, it could be because she'd skipped the larger breakfast she'd grown accustomed to. Leaving the ranch before the usual time Heath arrived meant she hadn't whipped up a hot meal. No matter. Josie had never enjoyed cooking for one. When Macy offered to pick her up for the day, Josie couldn't turn her down. Not when she wasn't sure if Heath would be stopping by.

*You could have called him.*

Absolutely not. She wasn't desperate. She had friends outside of Heath Grayson she could depend on. And she definitely didn't *need* that man.

She stretched and pressed her hand against her lower back as she adjusted how she was sitting. Abby, one of the housemothers, sat beside her, and Marnie, the ranch cook, occupied the other side of the table. The three women had spent the past hour decorating mason jars so they could be used as lanterns on the tables at the upcoming Thanksgiving celebration. Each one was covered in a strip of lace and then a Bible verse on linen was affixed on top of that. Twine circled the rim to form a rustic bow. Complete with flickering votive candles, scattered across the outdoor tables at the event as the sun sank lower, they'd be beautiful.

The rough wooden chair creaked under Josie's movements.

"Why don't you take a break?" Abby urged. "At least let me grab you another pillow to pad that seat. I can't imagine how uncomfortable crouching over all this small stuff is for you."

"I'm fine." Josie flexed her fingers and then reached for the next jar. "Let's get this done so we can cross it off the list."

"We have a week." Abby sighed. She snagged two more jars and the hot-glue gun.

Josie cut a length of lace to fit around the outside of the jar. "*Only* a week. I saw the list. It's long."

Marnie opened a second bag of votive candles and spread them along the center of the table, where they'd be easy to grab. "Speaking of lists, I'm finalizing the menu and compiling what I need for the final grocery run this weekend. Can I still count on your Ranger to be there?"

*He'll never be my Ranger.* Even though it was true, the words lodged themselves in Josie's throat. She looked down and fiddled with the strip of lace in her hand. So beautiful. So delicate. So easily destroyed if it was handled incorrectly or glued on wrong.

She ran the slightly frayed edge back and forth over her fingertips. "I'm…I'm not certain. I think so. He said he was, but…" She shrugged.

When she and Heath had met with Gabe to relay the

story about Avery, Josie's heart had swelled. They were a team—a good one. Hope had surged through her veins like a galloping horse set free in a new pasture. He'd taken her hand when she was upset. Reached over and had known that was what she needed without her even looking his way.

Dale had never acted like that.

For more than two weeks, Heath had done the chores around her ranch, shared her breakfast table and acted as her personal chauffeur. He'd sat beside her for the long haul in the waiting room yesterday.

Then disappeared last night after they talked to Gabe.

Why?

The piece of lace trembled in her hands.

It didn't matter. Heath didn't matter.

How had she let herself get so involved? So attached? When push came to shove, what did she really know about that man? Not much, other than his role in law enforcement, which was enough to make the achy feeling over his absence yesterday completely irrational. Also, he was great with kids, kind, patient and honorable.

Josie blinked away the heat of tears.

Marnie pressed her lips together and watched Josie for a moment. "Oh, honey. You're allowed to care about him," she whispered.

Marnie was known to fancy herself a matchmaker when it came to the ranch staff and volunteers. The woman wouldn't be happy until all the singles were paired off. She could often be found bending the ears of the ranch hands, urging them to have some courage and ask one of the women on a date. Lately a mysterious matchmaker had been leaving notes and gifts.

Whoever it was had successfully paired up the librarian, Macy, and the vice president of their chapter of the Lone Star Cowboy League, Tanner. They'd also had a hand in breaking up Tanner's sister's engagement and finding her a more deserving man. There was a rumor that Marnie was behind some of the obvious matchmaking attempts, but Josie wasn't so sure the cook would go as far as writing fake love notes or splitting up couples.

Then again, who knew?

If the woman was behind the hoopla, Josie would make sure Marnie understood she shouldn't involve her at all.

She took a deep breath.

"No, actually." Josie let the lace flutter to the ground, where it would end up covered in dust. Unusable. She fisted her hands and pressed them into her thighs. "I don't care about him. I won't let that happen."

Abby laid her hand over one of Josie's fists.

The cook jerked back in disbelief. "Why ever not?"

Because a good wife would still be devastated over the loss of her husband. Because Heath was a Texas Ranger, which meant every single day spelled danger for him. Because already her heart throbbed with deep pain when she thought about him leaving.

"A million reasons."

Marnie shook her head real fast a few times. "Child, do you honestly believe you're not allowed to be happy in this life?" She ducked her head to catch Josie's gaze. "That God wants you to only know suffering? That you're allotted one go around at love and once that's done you're put on some back shelf for the rest of your life? 'Cause if you believe that, you're wrong."

"My husband was killed." Josie usually tried not to

say that out loud because it sounded like she was asking for pity, but sometimes there was no way around it.

"I know, honey. I'm so sorry you had to live through that. But—*living*—that's the point. Despite what has happened, God is not done working in your life." She tapped the table a few times as she spoke. "Praise Him for that, honey. He's still doing a work in you. Don't make the mistake of punishing yourself for what happened, or holding back the growth God wants to bring into your life because you somehow believe you're undeserving of it." Marnie leaned over the table. "Don't go missing the blessings and opportunities He's laying out before you. They don't always come around again after we ignore them."

Josie cradled her stomach. "It was only six months ago."

The oven pinged. Marnie pressed up from the table and hustled over to pull the banana bread out. "There's no time stamp on these things. No rule books."

The baby moved. A foot or elbow pressed against Josie's hand. Hope and responsibility declared war on each other in her heart. She had to make wise choices for her child's future.

She took a shaky breath. "If I do end up falling in love again, it won't be with a Texas Ranger. That's for sure. I'm not risking my heart or my baby's future like that."

"Well, now." Marnie eased the steaming bread from the pan and set it to cool on a wide cutting board. "The Lord does often choose to work in mysterious ways. His ways aren't ours. Not ever."

Abby sorted through the stack of verses she'd carefully been writing on the linen sheets in her calligraphy-like handwriting. "Here it is. I think this is the one you need on your next jar." She handed over a verse.

Josie stared down at the strip of fabric.

*The joy of the Lord is my strength.*

Could that be true? Lately, Josie felt more beaten down than strong. What if her feelings were a result of her lack of joy? But no, it was natural to feel as she did after what she'd been through. Of course it was.

Josie set down the verse and slid back from the table. Her chair scraped along the ground. "You know, I think I do need to take a break and will stretch my legs a little after all."

Knowing she probably couldn't bend to pick it up anyway, she sidestepped the ruined piece of lace on the ground and tried to ignore the worried glance that passed between Marnie and Abby as she walked out the back door.

Heath poked his head through the opening in the barn door in search of Josie, but he spotted a lanky teen instead.

"Stephen?" Heath stepped into the room.

The teen startled and spun around to face him, a book clutched in his hands. "Wow. Okay. It's just you." Stephen gave a nervous laugh. "You scared me."

Heath scanned the area. Alone in the calf barn, Stephen had one of the pens unlatched. He'd been inside with the littlest calf, the one Josie liked to baby. The animal had markings that made it look like it had a white heart on its forehead. Everyone called it Honey.

What was Stephen up to? Simply reading? Heath hoped so. After spending time with the teenager, Heath's gut said Stephen was a good kid. But his police training demanded that he question the young man anyway.

"Where's Josie?"

Stephen gave Honey one last pat on the head and then stepped out of the pen. "Don't know." He checked the latch, making sure it was secure.

"She wasn't in here with you?"

"Just me." Stephen slipped the small paperback he carried into one of the back pockets of his jeans and then brushed his hands off on his thighs.

Heath strode forward, eating up the distance between them. "I never did get to ask you about the night someone set the calves free."

Stephen's eyes narrowed. "What would you need to ask me?"

Heath crossed his arms and widened his stance. "How I hear it, you were the only person unaccounted for that night. No alibi means you're the most likely suspect. At least, that's what it usually means."

The teen shoved his hands into the pocket on the front of his black hooded sweatshirt. "You've taught us enough in detection class—I know there has to be a motive. So, Officer…or whatever it is I should call you…what's my supposed motive? Why would I do something like that?"

"Because you…" Heath's eyes locked with the lanky teenager's and his tongue went dry. Anger, confusion, frustration, desperation—all there. Louder than all of it, though: *Believe in me.*

"Just say it. You know you want to." Stephen stalked forward. "I'm a bad person. I wouldn't be at this ranch if I wasn't. Right? And people like me will always do bad things. Since I got the label now, that's all I can be for the rest of my life. This is a place for bad seeds." He made finger quotes around the last words.

"Who told you that?" Heath asked gently.

"My stepfather." He jammed his hands back into the front pocket of his shirt. "It doesn't matter. You think it, too. Everyone thinks it." He jostled past Heath in the narrow area between the calf pens, shoulder checking him. Well…as hard as a scrawny teen could shoulder check a fit, thirty-year-old man.

With quick reflexes from ten years of needing them, Heath caught Stephen's arm and turned him back around before Stephen could take off. "Hey, listen. I don't think you're a bad person."

Stephen looked up at the ceiling, toward the wall, down at the floor, back up at the ceiling, anywhere in an attempt to hide the fact that he was about to cry. "Then what's my motive?" he ground out. "Why would I put our calves in danger? Huh?"

Heath laid his hand on Stephen's shoulder. "People do things when they're upset. Sometimes we're hurting and the pain takes over and we make choices we wish we hadn't. Because we're struggling and because life is hard. If that's what happened—it doesn't make you bad, okay?"

"How would you know anything?"

Heath hadn't been around for Nell or Flint when they needed him, and he had spent fifteen years closing off from everyone around him so they couldn't know the intimate parts of his life. From *knowing* him at all. But he could do this for Stephen. He could be there for him because opening up would be the brave thing to do.

And Heath didn't fancy himself a coward.

"My father died when I was fifteen. My mom remarried pretty quickly and my stepfather and I locked horns from day one." He dropped his hand from Stephen's shoulder. "He told me to buck up and stop moping about my dad."

Even fifteen years later, his stepfather's rejection still stung.

Heath leaned in. "Between you and me…I might have done some things to him that didn't help the situation. Nails in his tires, salt in his coffee when he asked for sugar, that sort of thing. I had a lot of anger and I just didn't know what to do with it." He straightened back up.

Might as well tell everything.

"In the end, he gave my mom an ultimatum—me or him. She chose him and I got shipped off to live at my uncle's ranch until I was old enough to join the army." He scrubbed his hand over his jaw. "So that's how I know. I made some choices fueled by hurt that I wish I hadn't. Things I can't explain the rationale behind, even now."

Stephen's Adam's apple bobbed. "Do you and him—your stepfather—are you two friends now?"

Heath shook his head. "I'm afraid we'll never be friends, but we can tolerate each other if we have to. So we do for my mother's sake. I wish I had a better picture to paint for you."

The teen toed at the ground. "My stepfather hates me."

"*Hate*'s a strong word." Heath sighed as he searched for the right way to explain things. "Men feel like a failure when they can't automatically fix something. A lot of men—we don't know how to connect and we're more afraid of failing than anything, so we don't try to work at a relationship, because walking away feels like a choice, whereas working at it and struggling feels like failing. It's not logical. But we men seldom are when it comes to relationships."

"So you're saying they point at us and say we're the problem so they don't have to invest and then feel like they can't fix us? It all comes down to pride?"

Heath nodded slowly. "I believe that's the case, and I'd be lying if I said I wasn't guilty of doing the same thing with people in my life."

Stephen finally made eye contact again. "Do you think the boys here are bad seeds?"

"Not anymore."

"I didn't set the calves free that night. I wouldn't do that."

"I believe you."

"I'm supposed to go home next month, for good." He fiddled with the cuff on his sleeve. "I don't want to. I don't want to live with him."

"Does your stepfather—does anyone lay a hand on you?" The muscles in Heath's back bunched up, tense. He'd fight tooth and nail to protect Stephen if he found out his stepfather was abusive.

"It's not like that. He doesn't hit me. He just makes it very obvious that he doesn't like me and doesn't think I'll measure up to anything."

"You're seventeen, son. One year." Heath held up a finger. He wished he could promise the teen that life would be wonderful when he went home to his parents. That they'd all get along great and make a ton of memories and his stepfather would be supportive. But Heath couldn't promise those things. False hope caused more pain in the world than outright punches. "You only have to stay for one year and then you'll be considered an adult and can strike out on your own if you have to. That's what I did."

"Will you… It's probably too much to ask." Stephen studied the toes of his gym shoes.

"Ask anyway."

"Would you help me? Mentor me, kind of…even after this month?"

A burning sensation filled Heath's chest, but it wasn't unpleasant. It was more of an ache than anything. A pain that had always been there but he hadn't recognized until that moment. Heath wanted to be a part of something—something more than just his career. He wanted to be actively involved in someone's life.

Heath coughed a little, clearing his throat. "Yeah, son. If you want me to, of course. I'll be in your life as long as you want me to be."

"Well, if that's the case." Stephen's face lit with a conspiratorial grin. "Want to help me get some hay down from the loft in the big barn? Flint asked me to do it an hour ago and he's going to come searching for me soon if I don't have that done before the next time he looks."

Heath laughed. "Oh, I see how it is." He turned to join Stephen but froze when he spotted Josie. She was leaning in the doorway. With her red hair braided and wearing jeans and a flannel shirt, she was the most beautiful person he'd ever laid eyes on. Every cell in his body told him to go over and hug her—at least apologize and make things right between them. But she might not appreciate having that talk in front of Stephen.

How much had she overheard?

She looked at Heath. "Will you come back here when you're done?"

*Always. I'll always come back to you. For as long as you'll let me.*

Where had that come from?

"Yes, ma'am." He tipped his hat. They had so much to say to each other, but none of it needed to be said in front of Stephen.

The teen slapped Heath on the back. "I'll send him back with hay for your calves, Ms. Josie."

She waved them out.

They headed toward the barn and climbed up into the loft. Heath scaled the huge pyramid of hay bales and passed the rectangles one by one to Stephen, who tossed them through the hole in the loft down into the main section of the barn.

Stephen moved, making the loft's floorboards groan. "You know, since I started your class, I notice things all the time. A lot more than I even realized there was to notice." Breathing heavy, he pointed at the tower of hay. "We probably only need one more."

Heath hefted the last bale toward Stephen. "And it's hard to turn your mind off once it starts."

"That's so true," Stephen grunted and tossed the bale down through the hole. "Like right now." He dusted off his hands. "This floor. The noise it makes." He stomped across the loft. "It's so different than the barn loft at the old ranch."

Heath stepped down from the hay, his legs suddenly wobbly. "How so?"

"That old one sounded…" Stephen screwed up his face. "I don't know…almost hollow."

"Hollow?" Heath's heartbeat sounded in his ears.

"Like there was space in between the levels." Stephen headed toward the ladder so he could climb down to the main level. "I'm probably wrong."

Heath licked his lips. Dare he hope? "Which barn, now, are you talking about?"

"The main one back at the old ranch."

The one where Dad was murdered.

# Chapter Nine

Josie prepared bottles for the calves and called over a few of the boys to move them out into the small pasture and take turns giving each calf a bottle. The boys were ecstatic—they always begged for the opportunity to do the bottle-feeding. By the time Heath strolled in with a bale of hay propped on his shoulder, Josie was alone again.

"Are they old enough to eat this stuff yet?" Heath swung down the bale and set it beside the cabinet where she stored the other food items.

She smiled and shook her head good-naturedly. Sure, Heath had told her he'd spent time on his uncle's ranch, but the man definitely had more city in him than country when it came to animal knowledge.

"We start them on hay at four days old. But they're mostly still on the bottle. If you must know, I end up sneaking most of it over to the goats." She pointed in the direction of the goat enclosure. "They're so cute and I've always wanted one. It's impossible to pass up their sweet little cries, so I feed them."

Heath tilted his head, wearing a soft smile. "You've always wanted a goat?"

"Or two." Josie laughed lightly. "I can't justify spending money to buy one now, but they're on the dream list for my ranch. Someday."

They stood for a moment, staring at each other. The man in front of her looked so capable, handsome and strong. She fought the powerful urge she felt to melt against him and beg him to change her mind about falling for a lawman.

What should she say? *Why did you leave yesterday without saying anything? Do you care about me? If not, why do you act like you do? Will you leave me...us... and never look back? Can I trust you?*

Heath cleared his throat. "I'm real sorry about leaving you stranded yesterday. That wasn't my intention. I was going to come back for you, but I should have told you that."

"Why'd you go?"

"To clear my head."

Of what? Of her? Of the ranch? "Did it work?"

A slight grin tugged at the corners of his lips. "Does it ever?"

Josie propped her hands on her sides. "I overheard what you said to Stephen."

He adjusted his hat. "All of it?"

"Most," she admitted. Okay, all. She happened to step through the doorway right as Heath began questioning the boy about the calf incident. "It was sweet of you to say you'd mentor him after November, but will you be able to do that?"

*Say you love it here. Say you're moving. Say you'll stay.*

"I don't live all that far. When assignments don't

take me away, I could swing by here in the evening if I wanted to." He propped his hand on the side of his belt.

"Stephen's scheduled to go home in December. He won't be here at the ranch any longer."

"Right." Heath scratched the back of his neck. "Cell phones and computers are wonderful inventions, as well."

"True, but they don't replace face-to-face interaction."

"I agree." He stepped closer. His voice was somewhere between a whisper and a breath. "Josie?"

Only her name—but the way he said it made her want to believe anything was possible.

She looked away. "You haven't told me much about your family. Will you?"

He stepped back and leaned against the wall. "What would you like to know?"

"Everything."

"You know more than most people already. I told you about my father. About my mother remarrying. You know about Nell and my niece. And you heard me tell Stephen about my stepfather."

Josie's heart twisted for the teenage boy who had lost his entire family in such a short time—his father in the line of duty and then his mother and sister because his mom chose his stepdad. Heath must have felt such anger toward the man. Suffered the slice of betrayal from his mother's actions. Known loneliness after being separated from his younger sister. All while mourning his hero. At least he and Nell had mended their fence.

"I can't believe your mother allowed him to kick you out." She laid her hand on his arm. The muscles under her touch were so solid and firm, much like the man, but she wanted to get past that to find out what drove him. "It wasn't fair of him to make that ultimatum."

He sighed. "She was still in mourning, too. My mom, she's not a strong woman—she's not like you. She'd never worked a day in her life and when my father died, she latched on to the first available man she could find. For security. Just to have someone to pay the bills and take care of her…at least that's how I saw it go down. I'm sure she figured she was doing it for us kids' sake, too. For me and Nell to have a father figure. It just didn't work out that way." He looked off to the side.

Josie squeezed his arm. "You're a good man, Heath. You've been through so much and were treated poorly by people who should have loved you and yet you're still so honorable. I don't know how you do it."

He looked down at her hand on his arm and exhaled. "Because of all that happened with my family, I don't… I don't know how to *show* people I care. A man my age should be able to do that. I'm starting to wonder if perhaps I'm not all that honorable after all."

She slid her hand down his arm to take his hand. "Hey, don't say that."

He wrapped his fingers over hers, clinging as if she was a lifeline. "What if everything I've done has been to prove my own worth? To prove that my dad would be proud of me and that my mom should have kept me? What if my drive has been wrong all along? Do you think that discounts everything I've done?"

She placed her other hand around their joined ones. "You're a good man. Do you hear me? Is that sinking in? I'll keep saying it if you need me to. I think you might be the best man I've ever known."

His deep brown eyes captured hers as he searched

her face. A hundred questions creased his brow. "I want to know you. Really know you. Tell me about your family, too."

Josie traced her thumb over his knuckles. "I'm an only child. My mother passed away when I was eleven. Brain tumor."

"I'm sorry," Heath whispered. He gently tugged her closer so they were sharing air as they spoke. The scent of fresh pine soap and hay dust enveloped her. If only he'd wrap his arms around her. She missed the feeling of being held more than she realized.

Josie took a deep breath, continuing, "Dale and I met my freshman year of high school. We never even officially dated—we met and he became my world. I was very young. I didn't know what I was looking for."

*I should have been searching for you.*

"My father was a truck driver, all over the country. He was gone a lot. I was lonely." She stopped tracing Heath's knuckles and let her hand rest on top of his. "Dale proposed the day after my eighteenth birthday. That same year my father's truck hit an icy patch in Colorado. His eighteen-wheeler went off the edge of the road into a ravine. They assured me he didn't feel any pain at the end."

With hesitation, Heath cupped his free hand around her shoulder blade. A fierce protective look crossed his face. Almost as if he never wanted to let go.

"You're all alone now, then, aren't you?"

"In a sense." She dipped her head. "But I'm not alone. Not really." Feeling bold because of their proximity, Josie tipped her face to his and whispered, "I'm not alone right now."

He sucked in a ragged breath. His gaze moved from

her eyes to her mouth, asking a question she didn't know how to answer.

She bit her lip. Change the subject. Before they both wound up doing something they'd regret. "Why won't you call your grandfather?"

Heath dropped her hand and turned, slipping around her from where he had been cornered between her and the wall. He yanked off his hat and tossed it on top of the feed cabinet, which made his hair stick up in adorable angles. He wrapped his hand over the back of his head. "When my mother remarried, we lost all connection to him, and when Nell and I tried to contact him later on, he hung up on us. I'm not so sure he wants to hear from me now."

"But you're going to try?"

"I promised I would, so I'll keep my word." He snatched his hat back up and worked it around and around in his hands. "Well, if you don't need me anymore, I better head out. There's something I need to go take a look at."

"Thanks for the hay," she called lamely as he left. The whole time holding back the words that desperately wanted to cross her lips.

*I need you, Heath Grayson. Wait. I'll always need you.*

Heath was afraid his heart was going to pound its way right through his rib cage.

*Calm down. Treat this like any other case.*

Impossible.

He turned his truck down the driveway that led to the area across town where the boys ranch had been located before Cyrus Culpepper left the Lone Star Cowboy League all his land. Heath knew this area of the old boys ranch well. He'd combed over it a handful of times during his friendship with Flint. Never in an official capacity before, because he'd only recently obtained clearance from his boss to investigate his father's cold case, but that hadn't stopped him from poking around. After all, it wasn't against the law for him to stumble upon clues off duty.

What had he missed?

Probably nothing. No doubt he was chasing the wind, but after Stephen's observation, he had to come back to check the barn.

*What if...?*

Heath had wanted to head to the old location right away, but talking with Josie had been more important. Before today, the crime scene sat for fifteen years— another half hour wasn't going to hurt it.

But a few more seconds with Josie? Oh, that would have changed everything. Heath groaned. He would have kissed her. Would Josie have responded favorably? She'd tilted her face up to his, as if to grant permission. He crammed his hat on. Focus. Right now he couldn't process all that. Not when he might finally have a lead after fifteen years of unanswered questions. He slammed the gear shift into Park and was out of his truck a second later, tearing his way toward the large barn. Flint had lent him the keys to the buildings, so getting through the locks wouldn't be a problem. He fished the ring of keys from his pocket.

For a minute he froze outside the side door. From the photos and case files back in his room at the inn, Heath knew he was standing exactly where his father had been murdered. They had found his body right here. No murder weapon. No reason for the killing.

Just gone.

The anniversary of his death was only four days away.

*You might be the best man I've ever met.*

"That's because you didn't know my father." Heath cupped his hand over his jaw. "He was the greatest man I've ever known." He squatted and pushed his fingertips into the hard ground. He blinked against a burning in his eyes.

Being at this location had never affected him in this way. Maybe Heath was going soft. Everything—the boys at the ranch, his family, realizing what a junk friend he'd been to Flint, and Josie, especially Josie—was making his chest sore from aching with emotions he'd never wanted to sort through before. From longing for a life he didn't know if he had the right to want.

He pressed his palm into the earth. "What did they do to you? Why did they do it?" But verbalizing questions wouldn't assist his investigation. His earthly dad was long past the point of being able to help him, but God—another Father—might be willing to help him, if only he'd ask.

Heath's knees hit the ground and he bowed his head. "God, I've left You out of all of this—haven't I? For the past fifteen years, I've set up cones around my dad's murder and told You to keep out. I *wanted* to hang on to that hurt. That's all I knew. It defined me."

He took a rattling breath. Might as well admit it all; God knew anyway. "And I've made every choice in my life to date because of it instead of seeking Your guidance. Forgive me, Lord. I've been so boorish. I've walked around saying I care about protecting people, when all I've done is make choices to protect myself—

my heart. Because of that, I've been a terrible witness for You. Haven't I? I've claimed Your name, claimed to follow You since I was a teen, but it was mostly in word and not deed. Exactly what I accused Flint and the League of doing in Josie's life. Well, no longer."

No one was around to see, so Heath tipped back his head and spread his arms as if he was opening them up to God. "I am Yours." He slowly rose to his feet. "My life is Yours. Guide my hands in this investigation. If there is justice, let it be because of You. I'm handing over my desire for vengeance to You. Heal me, Father. Please… I don't want to just exist anymore. I want to know a joy that comes from You. I want to live in a way that pleases You. In the name of Christ, I pray all these things." He opened his eyes and whispered, "Amen."

"Over here. This barn." Heath waved at Finn Brannigan, another Texas Ranger from Company F. On duty, Finn wore the normal Texas Ranger uniform—khaki pants, boots, a white button-down and his white Stetson. The gun on his hip glinted in the late-afternoon light.

Heath was surprised Finn answered the phone when he had called an hour ago. The man had recently gotten married and had taken an extended honeymoon, but apparently he was back to work now.

"Thanks for coming out so quickly." Heath extended his hand for a handshake. "How's married life?"

"If you get the opportunity, I highly recommend it." Finn pumped his hand once. "Amelia reminded me to thank you again for the wedding presents. She's planning to display both of them year-round."

Once Heath heard Amelia loved and collected Christmas decorations, he had enlisted his sister to pick out a wedding gift for them. Nell had tracked down a special Texas star for the top of their tree as well as an ornament in the shape of a pug in honor of Amelia's dog—Bug—who had played a role in bringing the couple together. Heath had felt cheesy giving the decorations to Finn and his bride, but the thoughtful gifts had struck a chord with Amelia. So far she'd thanked him three times in person, once in a thank-you card and had Finn thank him whenever their paths crossed.

"Come on in." Heath held open the barn door. "Let me show you what I found."

"What type of drugs?" Finn specialized in under-cover drug work, which was why Heath had called him. As much as Heath wanted to take the lead on his father's investigation, with what he'd uncovered in the barn, Finn was the better-trained man for the job. The best option was to let go of his desire to run the case and allow Finn to take over.

"Once I found them, I wasn't going to touch anything without another officer here. I didn't exactly bring evidence gloves and bags on my vacation. Let me show you." Heath climbed into the loft and walked to the far end until the sound the floorboards made changed. Slightly dull and hollow, just like Stephen had pointed out.

Finn's boots clomped behind him. "False floor?"

Heath nodded. "I don't know how it got missed in the original investigation." Then again, Heath had missed it the dozen times he'd scoped out that barn, as well.

The county offices were closed for the day, but with Finn's permission, tomorrow he would head over and uncover when the last building permits for the ranch had been submitted, and by whom. Of course, the perpetrator wouldn't have included the details about the false floor in whatever plans had been submitted for approval, but the boys ranch was frequented too often to alter the buildings without building permits. If they did, anybody could have reported them, and the drug-smuggling happening there would have been uncovered right away. Someone would have had to fake improvements or roll the false floor into approved plans to seamlessly achieve what they did. Heath would examine the building permits from fifteen years ago and follow the trail of names attached to the paperwork.

"Right here." Heath knelt down and pulled up the board that served as the way into the cubbyhole. The only difference between it and all the others was a slight, faded indent on the wood.

Finn crouched beside him and ran his hand along the floor. "No wonder it was never found. I can't say I would have spotted this. They constructed it in such a way that you can't tell from the lower level that there are two layers of floors up here. It's ingenious. I'm impressed. And with what I see every day, that's saying a lot."

"I thought the same thing." Heath lifted the board, revealing what looked like rows of tightly bundled bricks and a dusty Smith & Wesson .38 revolver.

Finn whistled and then pulled out a camera to begin photomapping the scene. "I'm itching to catalog everything, but I'm not about to risk muddying up the crime scene. We're going to have to call in the evidence crew to remove and package everything. The gun will have to go to the crime lab for prints. We won't know right away."

"I know. I do this all the time."

"For other people...not for the murder weapon in your dad's case."

Heath stared at the gun for a moment. That was what took his father's life. He was sure of that fact. Fifteen years without leads and all the answers had been here all along. A powerful feeling of peace and certainty pulsed through his veins. These items would lead to the killer. The angry teenager who still kicked around in his mind from time to time could finally rest.

Finn watched him. "Are you all right?"

"Relieved, more than anything. I want to move on from this." Heath gestured to encompass all the drugs. "If you had to guess, how much would you say is there?"

Finn cocked his head. "I'm assuming by the looks of it, there's both heroin and cocaine here. Combined, I'd say thirty to thirty-five kilograms." He narrowed his eyes, running a calculation in his head. "When all that's broken down for street use, it could be worth anywhere from a half million dollars to upward of one and a half million dollars. You're looking at what may end up being the biggest bust in my career."

A wave a nausea slammed into Heath as he rocked back to sit on his heels. "That... All of this... That's why they killed him. He must have been about to blow their cover." Heath swallowed hard. It was all so pointless. Drugs for his father's life. "But why leave it all here for fifteen years if they thought it was worth taking a man's life to hide?"

Finn punched a message into his phone, alerting the dispatch center to send the evidence technicians to their location. Neither man would disturb the possibly evidence-rich scene until the whole team was present and the correct tools were there.

"My assumption would be that whoever placed this here, and whoever killed to protect it, must have disappeared very soon after and hasn't been able to return since."

Unable to return for fifteen years? The obvious answer. "Jail?"

Finn nodded. "Either that or fled the country. There's also the possibility that the person could have died soon after killing your father. You need to prepare for that, should it be the case. Those are the only logical conclusions for abandoning a haul of this magnitude. At least it gives us a place to start."

Hopefully, it gave them not only the start—but the end, too.

# Chapter Ten

The baby was having a field day kicking at Josie's internal organs.

Josie braced her hand hard against her lower back. "I think the first lesson we'll focus on after you make your grand appearance is going to be manners. We don't kick vital organs that Mom might need later on. Hear that, lima bean?" She ran her hand over her stomach. The movement and subsequent pain subsided as she spoke. "There, now, isn't that so much better? Get some rest so all that energy can go into growing."

That morning Josie worked alongside Laura, one of the housemothers, changing all the bedsheets in the house before handing them over to the group of boys in charge of laundry that week.

Light as a butterfly, Laura touched Josie's shoulder. "Honey, maybe Bea's right. Maybe you should take it easier the closer it gets to your time. No one would blame you."

Although Josie recognized the wisdom and care behind Laura's words, the sentiment implying that Josie couldn't handle her load still ate at her. Sometimes in the evening when she was home alone, Josie would put on a documentary—one of her favorite pastimes. Pioneer women made meals and helped hoe fields *while in labor*; surely Josie was made of the same mettle. But she also recognized that people asked her to take it easy because they cared—not because they thought she was incapable.

It would take a long time to get over the beliefs Dale had spoken into her heart for years—ideas Josie now understood were wrong. *You can't do that. If you work, that makes me look bad. Even if we had a ranch, you wouldn't be able to handle the workload. It would fail.* Josie relaxed her hands. Dale had not been a horrible man. In fact, she'd loved her husband, but looking back objectively, she could recognize how controlling he'd been.

Now that she knew that, his leaving made sense—in a way. Dale had been a man who knew what he wanted in life and had done everything within his power to work toward a certain outcome. He cared deeply about what people thought of him. He loved wearing a badge because it made people instantly respect him. He hadn't wanted his wife to have a job because it might imply that he wasn't making enough money. And he'd wanted a family, a son to carry on his name…but he couldn't control if they became pregnant. That must have bothered him immensely.

The only thing within his control was the woman he was trying to have a family with. Josie had proven herself incapable of getting pregnant during their marriage, so Dale took control again and planned to leave.

Josie huffed and straightened her spine. "I still have three months. My doctor says I'm fine. It's not like I've been put on bed rest or something like that. A pain here and there is pretty normal, at least so say all the books and websites I've been reading."

"I understand. I was the same way with mine." Laura smiled at her. "But please, speak up if the tasks become too much for you."

They headed toward the kitchen area in the back of the ranch house and dark-haired Diego pounded through the back door. The second he spotted Josie, a smile overtook his face.

"There you are, Ms. Josie!" He crossed the room and hugged her middle.

She ruffled his thick hair. "I see someone's ready to check the calves."

"Ah, not just that." He grabbed her hand, tugging her toward the back door. "I like you a little, too."

Josie laughed. "So reassuring." She waved to Laura. "I guess this is my cue. See you later."

Outside, Diego let go of her hand and ran ahead of her by a few feet and then spun around. "I saw Ranger Heath today."

"Me, too."

"I know." Diego nodded, his eyes dancing. "You two show up together all the time." He stopped in front of her. "Are you two married?"

Josie let loose a nervous laugh and peeked around, hoping no one had overheard the loud boy. "No, of course not. Come on." She passed him.

He jogged to catch up. "Well, then, *when* are you two going to get married? Can I come to the wedding? Can I *be* in the wedding? I'll be so well behaved. If I have an itch or something, I won't even move. I promise. I'll stand still in all the pictures. I won't sneeze or anything. You'll be so proud, Ms. Josie. Will I still call you Ms. Josie after you get married? Or will it be Mrs. Josie…? Mrs. Heath? That don't sound right."

Exasperated that she couldn't get a word in, Josie let out a groan.

Diego stopped. His eyes went wide. "You okay, Ms. Josie? Is it the baby? Want me to go get Heath? He's just over by Flint." He pointed in the direction of the horse barn. "I'll get him."

Josie caught Diego's arm before he could take off. "No. Diego. Come back here. I'm fine. Completely fine." She—slowly—got on her knees so she could place her hands on the boy's shoulders and be eye level with him. "Ranger Heath and I aren't getting married. Okay? Whatever made you think we were?"

The boy scowled. "But don't you love each other?"

Did she…? She couldn't. She wouldn't let herself. But neither could she deny feelings, either.

Josie sighed. "I don't know how Heath feels."

The little boy's face went slack as if he was surprised that she didn't know something so obvious. "Then ask him."

Josie sat back on her heels. She'd regret getting on the ground later when she tried to stand. "Girls don't come right out and ask boys things like that."

"Then I'll ask him." Diego laid his hand over his heart.

Josie shook her head. "That's not how these things are done."

Besides, over breakfast Heath had told her about finding the drugs and revolver back at the old ranch site. A huge step toward solving his father's murder. If he was successful, Heath would be able to leave at the end of the month with that checked off his list. Done.

No need to ever return.

"Don't you like him?"

"I like him very much, but there's more to being married than just liking a person." Josie folded her hands in her lap and looked down at her fingers. "You have to think alike, have personalities and goals that complement each other, and more."

Diego crossed his arms and his eyebrows inched closer together. "It sounds like you're making it all harder than it needs to be. I seen how he looks at you and how you look when he's around. That's love, Ms. Josie. I think that's all you need."

Enough. She shouldn't involve an eight-year-old in her love life anyway. Or lack of a love life. She struggled to her feet. Diego offered her a hand and she held on to his shoulder as she stood.

Josie dusted off her jeans. "We aren't getting married."

"But your baby needs a daddy." Diego pointed at her stomach.

"Is that what this is about?"

"A lot of the boys here, we didn't grow up with dads." Diego kicked at a small rock buried mostly in the hard dirt. "You don't want your baby to grow up like that." He looked back up at Josie, eyes hopeful. "Heath would make a good dad."

Heath would make an excellent father and husband for a family someday. Some woman would be blessed to win his heart and devotion. Just not her.

Josie nodded slowly. "I agree with you there."

"But not for your baby?" The boy frowned and it twisted Josie's heart.

"He would have to want to be a daddy first." Josie opened the door to the barn and held her hand out, inviting Diego to go in first. "He's pretty focused on his job, and his job is very dangerous."

Diego brushed past her. "That makes him a hero."

"I think so." She headed toward the feed cabinet.

"You don't want to marry a hero?" Diego leaned down and gathered a few cattle brushes and combs into a bucket and then headed in the direction of the calf pens.

"Not don't. Can't," she whispered. She fanned her face, blinking away tears.

Stupid pregnancy emotions.

Josie reached to open the cabinet but stopped when she spotted a small bundle sitting on the counter. It hadn't been there earlier.

The printed label on the envelope read *For Josie*.

She tugged at the envelope, but it was heavily taped to the tissue-paper wrapping, so when she lifted the envelope, it ripped the paper open. Setting the card to the side, Josie ran her fingers over the pale yellow fabric poking through the hole in the tissue paper. Delightfully soft. Baby soft. She couldn't resist and tore off the rest of the paper. Two small stuffed animals tumbled onto the counter. A black-and-white grinning cow and a small brown goat with curly horns. Josie lightly touched the top of their little heads, one at a time. So adorable.

Whoever had left the gift knew about her love for cattle and goats.

Or perhaps they were an excellent guesser.

She pulled the yellow baby blanket from the package and snuggled it to her chest. Perfect. Josie imagined carrying her baby into her home in the blanket—safe and warm. She couldn't hold back her tears any longer. People at church and in the League had told her they were planning a baby shower, but this was the first gift she'd received for her baby. Everyone wanted to know the baby's gender, but Josie had chosen not to find out. She planned to decorate the tiny bedroom back at her dad's old fishing cabin yellow and gray. A barnyard theme had been on her mind, as well. It was almost as if whoever had left this gift knew that. Funny, though, she didn't remember ever telling anyone.

Josie set the gifts down and moved the tissue paper aside, searching for the envelope. Her fingers closed around the hard cardstock and she opened the clumsily taped-together seal on the back. A typed note fell out: *For your baby. From Heath Greyson.*

She bit back a smile.

As much as she wished it was from the man in question, Josie was fairly certain Heath would spell his own last name correctly. Which meant the ranch's mysterious matchmaker had their eye on Josie and Heath. Was the matchmaker Marnie Binder? Probably not. Marnie would have known how to spell Grayson. If Josie could figure it out, she'd loved to thank whoever had given her the thoughtful gifts.

Regardless, despite how much Josie fought her attraction to the man in law enforcement, imagining Heath giving her something like the stuffed animals and blanket made her smile even bigger.

Such foolishness.

Josie shook her head, folded the blanket into a tiny square and sat the stuffed animals on top.

Apparently she was spending too much time with Diego. He was filling her head with hopes, dreams and echoes of joy that were better left locked away, deep within her heart.

Heath trailed the boys in his detection class as they headed toward the learning center. They were done for the evening, but a handful of them had left their bags on the tables after finishing their homework assignments required by their teachers at the schools they attended in town.

He checked his phone for the seventh time.

No missed calls.

Last night, Finn and Heath had stayed on scene while the evidence technicians worked the area. Insisting that because Heath was on vacation, he shouldn't run around for the case, Finn had decided he'd follow up with the city's building department today to check on permits. Heath's coworker promised to call the moment he had news.

Letting go of his father's case might prove to be more difficult that Heath had originally thought.

He filled his lungs with the crisp, late November air. The sweet smell of cinnamon drifted from the kitchen. Marnie must be cooking up something amazing for dinner. Heath's stomach grumbled.

He pushed through the door and was met on the other side by five grinning boys.

Stephen slung his backpack over his shoulder. "Can I have a piece of your pie?"

"It looks really good," another boy chirped.

Heath swiveled his head to where they were all pointing. At the front of the reading area was a wide table. It was usually full of towering piles of books and paper-work, but presently it had been cleared off of all but a pie and a sheet of paper. Heath zigzagged through the group of boys to get to the table.

Not just any pie—a pumpkin pie, his favorite. Some-one had gone through a lot of work baking it and then decorating the top with swirls and cutouts of crust. He reached for the piece of computer paper beside it.

Stephen appeared at his elbow. "It's from Josie. Sorry. We already looked."

Heath raised an eyebrow at the boy.

Stephen shrugged. "Just putting our detection skills into practice."

"Investigating crimes and snooping in people's per-sonal affairs are two very different things." Heath nudged Stephen in his ribs good-naturedly.

Stephen grinned wickedly. "Maybe I want to be a PI. Can't you see it?" He spread out his hands as if envi-sioning his name in Broadway lights. "Stephen Barnes, Detective for Hire."

Heath pulled a face. "Most PIs are retired cops."

"Dream killer." Stephen playfully nudged Heath back. "Way to spoil my fun."

"Use your powers for good, Stephen." Heath winked at the teen.

Stephen laughed. Picking up on the hint, he rounded up the rest of the boys and ushered them out of the room. As he closed the door, he hollered, "But I was serious about you saving me a piece of pie, okay?"

"For good, Stephen."

"Pie, Heath. Remember my enduring love for pie." Stephen shut the door.

Heath chuckled. He'd sure miss ribbing with that

kid once the calendar changed to December. He turned back to the table and flipped the page over: *For Heath. Enjoy. —Josie M.*

It was impossible to hold back his grin. So, the lady *did* like him. After a near-silent ride to the ranch this morning, Heath was beginning to wonder if he had completely imagined their almost kiss yesterday afternoon. When he told her he thought he was close to solving his father's murder, she'd been downright icy. Why wasn't she happy for him?

But perhaps the pie was a peace offering. Or a window to her true emotions.

Josie had a justifiable reason for having reservations about getting involved with a Texas Ranger, but Heath was beginning to feel like all the risk was worth it. Why not? No matter how long he searched, he'd never meet another woman with such a mix of determination, strength, compassion and beauty.

He tucked the note into his back pocket and picked up the pie.

Yes, stubborn man that he was, his heart had betrayed his tough resolve to never get involved with a woman. Heath was falling for Josie Markham. And if the pie was any indication, she just might feel the same way about him.

## *Chapter Eleven*

The goats called to Josie with wavering bleats as she passed their enclosure.

"Not now, sweethearts." She shifted the blanket and stuffed animals she was carrying into one arm so she could go down the row and pet each one. The smaller goats had their heads at odd angles, completely rammed through the wires of the fence, while the larger ones braced their front hooves on the groove of the fence, making them tall enough to stick their heads over the top line. The coarse hair of their whiskers tickled her skin.

"I'll sneak you goodies later, though. I promise."

Thankfully, bucks weren't kept with the herd, so Josie didn't have to contend with the reek of the male goats, which was worse in the fall. Her pregnant nose couldn't have handled the bucks right now. However, the wethers and does were delightful. Each one nuzzled at her hand, their large eyes following her every movement as if she might still have treats on her somewhere and she was holding out on them. Dale used to say goats creeped him out because their eyes looked like something out of a science-fiction movie, but their strange eyes, with the rectangular pupils, were one of the reasons Josie found them so charming.

"Those are cute." Katie Ellis, the receptionist at the boys ranch, pointed at the stuffed animals and blanket in Josie's arms as the two women met halfway up the walk to the back door of the giant ranch house. Her curly blond hair looked extra bouncy today, and was it only Josie's imagination, or was Katie sporting some new makeup? Her green eyes really popped.

"Not the goats. The stuffed animals. Where are they from?" Her face read blank and Josie knew she wasn't that good of an actress. Katie Ellis was definitely not the mystery matchmaker.

Should Josie bother with telling her about the fake note? Sometimes Katie had a way of over-romanticizing situations. After Diego's questions about marriage, Josie wasn't sure she was up for more matchmaking talk.

Josie shifted to cradle the items in both hands. "I was hoping you might know. Someone left them for me."

"No tag?"

Not a tag Josie believed. "You could say that."

Katie glanced at the stuffed cow. "Aww. That's supercute." She handed over a canvas shopping bag. "Here. Take my bag. I insist. I was using the excuse of tossing this in my car as a way to get a breath of fresh air anyway." Katie pivoted to face the side yard as she talked.

Josie followed her movements to where Andrew Walsh, the extremely young but devoted senior pastor of Haven Community Church, was teaching a group of boys how to tend the compost heap—all in the name of a hands-on Bible lesson. Earlier he'd led the boys around the ranch until they returned with wheelbarrows loaded

down with fallen leaves and plant debris. Usually Josie
gave the compost area a wide berth. The musty, rotting
smell that wafted from the heap was enough to make
her nauseous for the rest of the day.

"That's expertly done, Sam." Pastor Walsh clapped
one of the quieter boys on the back in an encouraging
manner. "Dry materials, green matter, a shovelful of
soil and a sprinkling of fertilizer. Mix. Repeat. You remembered that all on your own."

Young Jasper—who was known as the ranch prank-
ster—snickered beneath his mop of sandy-brown hair.
"And by fertilizer, he means horse—"

"Now, now, Jasper. We all know what it really is."
Andrew intercepted the conversation before it went
south. The pastor excelled at redirecting the boys. He
turned back to the others waiting in line. "Fertilizer actually teaches us an important spiritual lesson."

More of the boys joined Jasper's laugher.

"Believe me, I know. I know." Andrew shook his
head in a commiserating way. "As funny as it sounds,
sometimes it's a good thing when we can draw spiritual
parallels from the most mundane items. If we connect
something we see or experience daily with a spiritual
lesson, it teaches our minds to see God's hand everywhere." Andrew didn't look fazed by their continued
stream of giggles.

"Even with—" Jasper doubled over before he could
finish his question.

"Even with fertilizer." Pastor Walsh ruffled the boy's
already unruly hair. "Because fertilizer teaches us that
it's not where we begin that matters—we all have the
power to work toward enriching the future. You do."
He laid his hand on top of little Morgan Duff's head.

"And I do, too." He placed his hand over his chest and kept moving. "It's our job to discover the skills and passions God has placed within us and then use those to better and grow His Kingdom. That's something each and every one of us is called to do. No exceptions. Even if in the beginning of our journey we feel like we have the potential of…fertilizer."

"Even me?" Sam asked. "Or is that just for pastors?"

"Especially you." Pastor Walsh's voice was warm. "Isn't that exciting?"

Jasper draped his arm over Sam's shoulders. "Yeah, it starts as hay and ends up as—"

Andrew cleared his throat. "I believe it's your turn, Jasper."

Josie adjusted her hold on the canvas bag and then reached over and squeezed Katie's arm. "So by *fresh air* you really meant you needed an excuse to venture outside to spy on poor Pastor Walsh?"

Katie gasped. "Am I really that obvious?"

Josie shook her head in an *I can't believe you don't know already* way. "Only to everyone."

Katie tilted her head and smiled dreamily. "Isn't he so wonderful with the boys?"

Josie nodded. "He really does have a way of connecting with them and I've never seen him get exasperated with any of them…not even Jasper. I don't think anyone else on the ranch can say that for themselves."

The younger woman sighed. "I wish he would ask me out already. Better yet, I wish the ranch matchmaker would start trying to pair us up."

Josie looped her arm through Katie's and turned her to walk away from the ranch house, in the direction of the red barn. "Speaking of the ranch matchmaker…any rumblings? I haven't heard the latest hypothesis. Do we have any idea who it is?"

"Are you kidding? If I knew, I'd be begging them about Andrew."

"Right." Of course.

"Oh!" Katie's eyebrows shot up toward her hairline. "You think the matchmaker sent you that gift?"

"I don't think. I know." Josie fished the typed card from the bag and handed it over. "See." She tapped the card. "His last name is spelled wrong. I doubt Heath would do that."

"*E* and *A* aren't *that* far from each other on the keyboard."

"Far enough."

Katie fanned the card. "You know, whoever the matchmaker is…he or she has been successful with every couple so far. You might as well give in and pick a date for the wedding."

Leave it to Katie.

"Don't start." Josie snatched back the card. "Anyway, so far it's only been Tanner and Macy, and they complement each other well. I'm sure they would have ended up together without the matchmaker's interference."

"Not true." Katie pursed her lips and wagged her head back and forth. "The matchmaker also broke up Chloe's engagement."

Josie couldn't argue that point. Tanner's sister wouldn't have discovered her fiancé's cheating ways unless the matchmaker had steered her in the right direction.

"But Chloe's fiancé was a creep. That would have come out sooner or later." Or not…but it burned Josie to give the matchmaker any more credit now that whoever was behind the letters was twisting her heart with hope about Heath.

"Well, well, lookie who we have here." Katie winked at Josie and then jutted her head to the side. Heath was cutting his way across the barnyard, heading straight toward Josie.

"I'll take this as my signal to go back to my desk. But between you and me—" Katie leaned closer, speaking at a loud whisper "—I may or may not walk *really, really slowly* past the compost bin."

"You're incorrigible," Josie called after her retreating figure.

Heath stopped a pace away and chuckled. "Me? Or her?"

Josie sighed in a good-natured way. "Probably both of you."

She met his deep gaze and rocked forward onto her toes. Looking into his eyes gave her the feeling of tipping over, headfirst, diving. And she found, in the moment, she didn't mind that feeling.

Not one bit.

Josie's brown eyes were warm and inviting as she joked with him.

Not just falling…nope… He was 100 percent, entirely in love with her.

There.

Had that been so hard to admit?

Heath should have kissed her yesterday. He wanted to right at that moment, but they were out in the open, and even if Josie welcomed the advance, she probably wouldn't want a display of affection to happen in such a public manner.

At least not the first time.

Heath had the pie balanced in one hand. He looked down at the pie and back at Josie. Then back at the pie. *Well, talk already.* But he wasn't quite sure how to start the conversation. The past few days had felt like they were playing tug-of-war. One second he thought Josie cared about him and the next she was silent and withdrawn. Then the pie.

He lifted the pie so it was right between them. "I know over the past few days we've experienced a couple of miscommunications, but I wanted to say thank-you. I really appreciate this gesture."

Her brow formed a V. "I'm sorry, but what gesture? I have no idea what you're referring to." Josie crossed her arms, a reusable grocery bag hung around one of her wrists so it dangled over her stomach. "And it's not even noon—why are you carrying around a pie?"

He jerked his head back. Was she joking? If someone was pulling a prank on Heath, they were cruel. He'd taken the pie to believe she cared about him. Apparently he was a fool.

Heath looked down at the pie as if it held the answer. "Because you gave it to me?"

"I didn't."

Suddenly the pie felt very heavy. He lowered his arm. "You left it for me, but you didn't make it. Is that it?"

"I have never seen that pie before in my life."

"Color me confused, then." Heath pulled the printer paper with Josie's note from his back pocket and handed it to her.

Josie glanced at the page and then tipped back her head and belly laughed. Not exactly the response he had hoped for. It would have been better if she'd looked at it and said, *Oh, this? I'd forgotten I wrote it. Yeah, it was me. I'm actually in love with you. Want to eat pie and be together forever?* If a man didn't have hope, he had nothing.

A stiff wind ripped across the ranch, shooting dust like pellets against Heath's back. Hopefully, the wind meant rain was in the air. The ground could use it. So could everyone's sinuses.

Josie groaned. "I should have known."

Heath rocked forward in his boots. "I'm usually pretty quick on the uptake…but I feel like I'm missing something here."

Josie's lips quivered as she tried to hide a teasing smile. "Are you completely certain you're a trained detective? Because…" The grin that tiptoed across her lips was downright mischievous. Heath loved seeing Josie's playful side. If he was going to be the butt of a joke, at least he got to flirt with Josie in the meantime.

"Give me that." He snatched the page back.

Josie held up a finger. "One, why would I type a note that short?"

"Maybe because you have terrible handwriting."

She opened her mouth and her eyes went wide.

He held up his hand. "Oh, I've seen it. With that handwriting, you could be a doctor, sweetheart." He folded the page into a small square and tucked it safely into the back pocket of his jeans.

"Two," Josie continued, obviously enjoying the back-and-forth jabs, "why sign it with the initial to my last name? I'm the only Josie here."

"I don't know." He tossed up his free hand. "I saw pie. I thought, *That's really nice.* My mind was clouded by pie."

She giggled. "Three, there's this." She fished a small card out of her bag and handed it to him. It was a note from him...a fake note. Heath hadn't written it. Although, now he wished he'd been smart enough to have the idea of giving her a gift.

"Well, now, this is downright ridiculous. They spelled my name wrong." He raised his voice in mock offense.

It was her turn to snatch back the card. "That's how I knew it was a fake right away."

"So what did I supposedly give you?" He craned his neck to try to look into the bag.

Josie showed him two small stuffed animals and a tiny blanket. "Isn't this little goat the cutest thing?"

"I'm not an expert in cute—they don't train us on that in the academy—but I will say, are you sure that's a blanket and not a washcloth? It's almost nonexistent."

She traced her fingers over the plush fabric. "Babies are exactly this size in the beginning. You'll see."

Babies were awfully small when they first entered the world, weren't they? Heath's gut bunched into a knot. Josie would need someone helping her more than ever once March hit. He imagined her and him relaxing on the couch back at her ranch after a full dinner, a tiny yellow blanket spread between them with a baby sleeping soundly as they both watched on.

She had said *You'll see...* Did she mean it?

Heath cleared his throat as well as the image from his head. "It was very nice of me to give you that."

"Incredibly thoughtful." She tucked the stuffed animals back into the bag.

She hadn't given him the pie. So what? He could still try to find out if she had any interest in him beyond someone who was fixing the fence at her ranch for free. Besides a chauffeur.

Heath balanced the pie on the top of a fence post and then touched Josie on the arm. "If you have a second, I think we need to talk."

Josie's smile dissolved. "Aren't we talking now?"

Although they were out in the open, Heath closed the distance between them so no one could overhear. "I understand—it's only been six months. I know you're still in love with your...with..."

"My late husband," Josie offered.

Heath swallowed hard. Nodded.

Josie bowed her head. "He was planning to leave me," she whispered. "That's the twist no one knows about." She angled her face a bit to be able to meet his eyes. "Just me, and now you. The day before...before he was shot, that's the day he told me he was walking out on our marriage."

The word *twist* couldn't have been used more appropriately.

Heath had a hard time wrapping his head around the idea of a man being stupid enough to leave a woman as amazing as Josie. "Are you sure?"

"He'd packed up all his belongings." Josie suddenly gripped Heath's arm, as if without him she might not be able to stand. "He already had a divorce attorney lined up."

Heath caught Flint eyeing them from across the barnyard. No doubt, his friend would have some severe words for him after seeing them together. But Flint didn't get it. It was impossible for Heath to stay away from Josie.

"Josie." Heath fought the desire to wrap his arms around her.

She pulled her hand away from him and tucked it against her side, giving herself the hug he wanted to offer. "I hear it happens to a lot of spouses in law enforcement."

"Not everyone. I know countless guys in happy marriages who adore their wives. Guys in my company."

Josie shrugged and blinked a whole bunch of times. "He wanted a child. That's the real kicker to my sad little story. He said I couldn't give him what he wanted. I was pregnant, Heath." She laughed once, but it held no humor. "I didn't know it yet, but he was leaving me and I was standing there crying with our baby growing the whole time." She hugged her stomach even tighter. "At least I know this little one was wanted. Even if I wasn't."

*I want you. I'll always want you.*

Heath fisted his hand. His muscles screamed for an outlet—something to punch—some way to burn off the anger he felt for how Josie had been treated. He forced his fingers to straighten, flex again, straighten. No fists, but his voice shook. "I mean no disrespect to your husband's death or his office, but in this, he was a fool."

"I'm not in love with Dale anymore," she whispered. "That's all I meant to say."

"Josie." His voice was only a breath. A breath that held every hope for the future. Could she hear it?

She turned so he could no longer see her face. "You had a breakthrough on your father's case yesterday. If you solve it, will you be leaving before Thanksgiving?"

"Flint still wants me to look into the run of incidents

happening here. The thefts and the animals being set loose."

Josie gave him a look that said *level with me*. "You've been poking around and asking everyone questions all month. No offense, but I think we both know that investigation is going to come to nothing."

Heath ran his fingers over his jaw. "Some people are suggesting I should question a man named Fletcher Snowden Phillips."

Josie rolled her eyes. "Fletcher's a pain, but I doubt he'd do anything illegal. Besides, this isn't what I wanted to talk about—you were always here for your dad's case. If you solve it, will you leave?"

Did she want him gone? "Do you want me to?"

"That's not what I asked."

He came beside her. "I'm more interested in that answer, though."

"You're a pest." She looked up and shook her head, but she lacked the smile that usually completed the gesture. "You know that, right?"

"I believe you told me so on the first day we met," he added softly.

"My opinion of you hasn't changed, then."

For a man who specialized in reading conversations and directing them so he got the answers he needed, Heath was having a hard time knowing the right words to say. Josie seemed to want to steer all talk away from where he'd been headed. She didn't want a relationship with him, did she? They could tease each other, they could help each other, but she was putting a stop on any paths toward romance. Every time he hinted at caring about her, she brought up the fact that he was leaving soon. As if she wanted to constantly remind him that there was no hope for them as a couple.

Fine. He was man enough to respect that. His heart wouldn't, but he could keep his distance, for her sake.

Heath worked his jaw back and forth. Took a deep breath. "I'll consider that a good thing, then. At least your opinion of me hasn't gotten worse. So there's that."

"How long, Heath?" She faced him. "How long will you actually be around?"

*What do you want? Just say what you want. Give me a clue.* He searched her face.

His phone rang. He automatically yanked it from his pocket and glanced at the screen. Finn. It would be news about Dad's case. He looked back at Josie.

She sighed and batted her hand. "Take the call. That's what you're here for. Take it."

He hesitated, but pressed Accept. "You got news?"

"Better than news. I think I found our guy."

When he hung up, Josie was already halfway up the walk to the ranch house.

# Chapter Twelve

A hard wind shoved against Heath's door as he stepped out of his truck and scanned the parking lot at the McLennan County Jail facility for Finn. The building, with its tan stonework, stood like a sentry, tall, cold and imposing.

So this was it.

Finn waited near the front of the entrance used by law enforcement. He'd set up a meeting with an inmate by the name of Kane Grubbs. Heath had glanced over Grubbs's arrest record. The man was serving time for a string of both financial and physical crimes. His original arrest dated back to the week after Heath's father was murdered. Each time Grubbs was released, he committed another crime and quickly returned to prison. During his latest arrest, he'd battered an officer and removed his weapon during the altercation—not something authorities took lightly.

In the past twenty-four hours, Finn had poked around for more information and everything he'd learned pointed to Grubbs being their man. It turned out Grubbs had worked at the boys ranch off and on during the time that Heath's father was murdered; he'd spearheaded the renovations to the barn and insisted on doing the construction work on his own for free.

Finn had his smartphone pressed to his ear and his voice carried. "That sounds good for tonight. I shouldn't be long. I love you, too."

Heath hung back until Finn was done, but when he overheard his coworker's conversation, Heath couldn't help thinking about Josie again. It would be nice to be able to talk openly with that woman, but Finn and Amelia were married, vowed to each other, so they had the right. Heath didn't.

Maybe it was for the best that Heath told himself long ago that he'd never get involved with a woman because of his job. Better that way. Because women and love were more confusing than any case he'd ever worked. He wasn't cut out for romance.

Finn stowed his phone. "You ready?"

Nope. Not for the interview or for Josie.

Heath stayed rooted in his spot. "Before we go in, can I...ah...can I ask you a personal question?"

Finn stretched his back, making his shoulders pop. "If it was my father, I'd want to know."

"It's not about the case." Heath almost lost the nerve to ask him, but he had to. No telling how much time would pass before he had another opportunity to ask a married lawman for relationship advice.

"Sure...go ahead and ask."

"Even with our job being as dangerous as it is, you were married before—and chose to marry again." Heath rested his hands on the edge of his bulky Ranger belt. "I guess I wonder why. Each day we walk into situations we might not walk out of. Why take the risk?"

Finn's chest lifted with a huge breath. He looked off at the clouds for so long, Heath began to wonder if he'd answer him at all. Were his questions offensive?

"I lost my first wife and my daughter," Finn said. "That was… Going through that is unimaginable and it's impossible to explain that kind of pain." Finn held up his hand. "But I don't regret having loved them for a second. They're gone and I—with the dangerous job, as you put it—am the one who was left behind."

"But level with me." Heath pushed the issue—he needed a solid answer. Something to help order his thoughts. "It crosses our mind every time we rush into a warehouse with our guns out. What-ifs are there for all of us, but I have to imagine that a married man has double the what-ifs to consider than someone like me."

"You're not wrong, but the real question is—are the what-ifs worth it to you? A married man and a man with children carry much more into a battle, but if you think about it, they're also fighting for something greater, too." Finn frowned a little. "Do you trust God, Heath? Do you believe He has a hold on your life and cares about the people you love?"

"I…I *want* to trust God like that."

"If Amelia and I get one more day together or sixty more years, we'll treat each one as a gift. Because we're not guaranteed tomorrow in this life, Heath. And that's true no matter if you're a butcher or a baker or a rancher or a Texas Ranger." In an uncharacteristic move, Finn rested his hand on Heath's shoulder. "I'll say this and then leave it be—if you love someone, do something about it. Today. Having that love today is worth the risk of having it ripped away tomorrow. I promise you that."

* * *

On the way back to the ranch, Josie would buy a cupcake for Katie at the bakery in town to thank her for the use of her car.

Josie parked on the edge of the path. That was the thing about cemeteries, they didn't have parking spots. People weren't meant to stay long.

Pastor Walsh had advised her to go to Dale's grave site and make peace with his death. He instructed her to talk out loud if she needed to. And to pray.

It would be her third visit since the funeral, but that day rushed back all at once. Bagpipes playing "Amazing Grace," the entire sheriff's department saluting in their dress blues, huge displays of fresh flowers crowding the funeral home—the smell of the bouquets mixing with everyone's over-applied perfumes.

Why did people feel the need to wear perfume or cologne to a funeral? Who were they worried about impressing? The deceased didn't care how they smelled and the family wouldn't even notice. Josie shook her head.

She could still feel all the hugs and hear the whispered *I'm sorry for your loss* from strangers who would never speak to her again or be there with her as she tried to piece her life back together. She could still hear the final call for Dale's badge number over the loudspeaker, a call that would forever go unanswered—a law-enforcement tradition.

On shaky legs, she stepped out of the car and headed toward Dale's headstone. Josie stopped a few feet away and crossed her arms. It felt futile, coming to speak to a grave, but she knew she needed to get the words out. If she didn't process everything she'd been feeling over the past six months, she'd never be able to move on. And Josie wanted to be able to do that—move on—desperately. For her child's sake, if not her own.

"I don't really know what I'm supposed to say right now." She traced her fingers up and down her arms, but it only left her feeling colder. "I'm pregnant. We're going to have a child."

Josie took another step closer. "Actually, I do have something to say. I'm mad at you. I'm as mad at you today as I would be if you were standing here alive." She clenched her hands into fists. "I'm mad because you wanted to leave me. Because I wasn't enough for you."

Her throat caught with tears and she couldn't see through the blur in her eyes anymore. "I'm mad that you didn't love me enough to stay even if we were never going to have a child. You never believed in me—never encouraged my dreams. How hard would that have been?"

She took another step closer, her words tumbling out faster. "I'm furious about the financial situation you left me in. Why were you gambling? What were you trying to prove by racking up so much debt? Why didn't you pay our taxes? I trusted you to do that. You were an officer! Not paying taxes is illegal."

Her chest ached. It was best not to ask questions. She'd never get the answers she wanted. "But I'm also mad that you died. I'm mad that you're gone and I'm alone. I'm mad I didn't get to see if we could have saved our marriage."

Her arms were shaking now. Her voice, too. "But now I'm done being mad." She swiped at her cheeks. "For the past six months, I've carried around guilt— as if I was to blame for you leaving. As if I should be ashamed for not being *enough* for you." Her voice broke on a sob. "But you know what? Leaving was your choice. Not mine. You promised to love and cherish me forever, but instead you gave up. I won't blame myself for that anymore. I am not responsible for carrying your mistakes."

Josie rested her head in her hands and took a few breaths. While she did not regret the years she was married to him, she'd come to the realization that Dale had made all the choices in their life—in her life. Forgiving Dale was the final step to no longer being controlled by him.

"You were my husband—my first love—and I miss you," Josie whispered. "I forgive you for giving up on us. I forgive you for everything."

Feeling light-headed, she staggered back to the car and dropped into the driver's seat. If she wasn't pregnant, she would have stayed and prayed at the grave site, but getting up from the ground was difficult.

"God," Josie prayed as she rested her head on the steering wheel. "Renew my heart and my spirit. I feel like I've been an old, threadbare version of the woman I'm supposed to be for a long time. I've been running on spiritual fumes, and I don't want to live like that anymore. I want to be full of Your love and joy. I want people to meet me and automatically see You in how I act and speak. I don't know what my next step is, but I know You do. Guide me? Show me what to do where Heath is concerned. I'm afraid to be a mother alone, but if that's Your will for me, I know You'll equip me for the task. No matter what I've walked through or who has left me, I know You've always been there. Thank You, Jesus. Amen."

Josie turned the key and headed toward town.

Even with forgiveness, many of Dale's bad choices still affected Josie's life. But she was no longer going to allow the wrong he'd done to have power over her.

She gripped the wheel tighter as light rain started to patter against the windshield.

Now Josie was in charge of the choices in her life—which also meant that she would be to blame if she made the wrong decisions. What was she going to do about Heath? She hadn't wanted to be involved with a man in law enforcement again, but whether or not they admitted to it, weren't they already involved? She looked forward to every minute spent in his company. But what if those minutes ended tomorrow because of his job? She had to think of her baby. Her baby needed a father who would be there to dance at his or her wedding, to hold grandchildren.

Then again... What if—like Dale—Josie was walking away from someone without realizing the life and joy that was already growing between them?

No matter where Heath traveled, every prison was the same.

Poured-concrete floors made footfalls sound hollow. There was the constant shriek of metal grating against metal and the smell of stale, humid recirculated air. Finn was ahead of him, talking with one of the guards as they passed down a long corridor on the way to the interview room. A strong bleach smell did very little to cover up a lingering trace of grease, dirty mop water and, oddly, an overwhelming scent of corn chips that permeated the space.

The guard showed them into the interview room. "I'll get Grubbs."

Finn joined Heath at the steel table in the center of the area. "Are you ready for this?"

"I don't think not being ready is an option."

A buzzer sounded, letting them know the guards were bringing in a prisoner. The door opened and Heath looked up—meeting the eyes of the man who most likely killed his father, or at least knew who killed him.

Over the years, Heath had wondered how he'd react if he ever found the murderer. He thought he'd feel rage. He thought he would want to slam the guy against a wall.

But it was pity drying the back of his throat, making it difficult to swallow.

Thin, bald and pale, Kane Grubbs needed a guard on either side of him, holding his arms, to help him shuffle in. The prison-issued jumpsuit, which looked like it was the smallest size they probably offered, hung off his body. One of the guards wheeled an IV unit beside Grubbs, and a woman wearing scrubs filed into the room.

Heath glanced over at Finn, but his face remained unreadable.

Grubbs slowly eased into the seat across from them. His shoulders shuddered violently as he hacked a few times. Heath studied him, trying to place his age. Grubbs wheezed in a breath, folded his hands on the table and then looked up at Heath. The whites of his eyes had a yellow tint to them.

"I know why you're here." He coughed again.

Finn nodded and pulled paperwork out of his manila folder. He read Grubbs his Miranda rights and then slid the sheet across the table. "Please initial each line and sign at the bottom, saying you understand. Also, I need to remind you that this room is being both video and audio recorded at all times."

Grubbs nodded by a fraction and signed the sheet. Then he looked back at Heath. "You look just like him. Your pa."

Heath's heart pounded as loud as a metronome. He opened his mouth. Closed it. "You... Did you know my father?"

The prisoner cradled his arms together. His chair creaked loudly as he rocked back and forth. "If you can't tell, I'm dying. Stage four. They say the cancer's everywhere. Two months left, if that. Being that I'm here, it could be tomorrow."

Heath's stomach rolled. "I'm sorry to hear that."

"Are you, now? We'll see if that sticks." Grubbs stopped rocking. For a few moments, the only sound in the room was the tick of his IV. "I have nothing to hide. Death on your back will do that to a body. I know you look like your pa because I was the last one to see him. I pulled the trigger. I killed him. If you located my hiding spot, you'll find my fingerprints on the gun."

Although Heath had suspected as much, hearing it confirmed ripped through him with a sharp, physical pain. He hunched his shoulders and shoved his fist against his chest.

"*Why?* He had two children. I was fifteen." His tone wasn't professional, but that was because the Texas Ranger wasn't talking; the boy who'd lost his hero was.

Grubbs flattened his hands on the surface of the cold metal table. "He got in the way of my lucrative business. It's as simple and complicated as that."

Finn cleared his throat. "Heath? A minute, please?" He motioned toward the doors and told the guards he'd be back shortly.

Legs trembling and heart blasting in his ears, Heath followed Finn out into the hallway. The second the door closed, Finn faced him. "This was a bad idea. Your being here. I'm going to get his written confession and finish the interview. I want you to be done with this case."

Heath's back hit the wall as his knees went wobbly. He bowed his head and pinched the bridge of his nose. "What does it matter? We're too late. The man's dying. It doesn't even matter anymore."

"You may not get retribution, but having an answer means closure. We'll change the cold-case label to Case Closed. *That* matters."

"The man's body is killing itself." Heath slammed his eyes shut and tipped his head back. He would not cry in the middle of a prison. "I don't need retribution. I just… I want to be done."

"And you are. I'll take it from here. I promise to treat this case as if it was my own family." Finn reached for the door handle, but then hesitated. "Are you all right to drive?"

"I'm fine. I just need a minute."

"Your father would be proud."

Not trusting his voice, Heath simply nodded. Finn headed back into the interview room, leaving Heath to slide down the wall until he was sitting on the floor.

It was done. He was done searching. Done making decisions for his life based on what happened to his father. Done living in fear, because if he was being honest, that was what most of his problems had been rooted in. Fear that he would never measure up to the man his father was. Fear that he'd never solve the case. Fear that his life didn't matter. Fear that he'd die, too. Fear that no one would miss him.

No more fear.

It was time for Heath to finally live.

## Chapter Thirteen

Heath sat in his truck, watching the workings of the boys ranch through the front window. He squinted. That was Tanner and Macy in the horse arena with a couple of the residents.

"Just call." Heath stared at the phone in his hand.

Today he was supposed to give Gabe an answer about his grandfather. Too bad he hadn't called yet.

Even if his grandfather chewed him out on the phone—it was only a phone—Heath could end the conversation at any time. The worst the old man could do was hang up, and he'd done that before, so Heath had nothing to worry about. He finally pressed the call button.

His grandfather answered by clearing his throat over the phone. "If this is one of you charities calling about donations, we aren't giving."

"Grandpa? It's me. Heath."

"I didn't recognize your number. Is it new?"

Would he have answered if he'd known who was on the other end?

Heath worked his jaw back and forth. "I've had this number for six years."

"I guess it's been a while since we talked."

"That it has."

"Did you get my card? I sent it a ways back."

"I did. Thank you." Heath collected his thoughts. What to address first? "I called for a couple of reasons, but mostly because I wanted you to know that my company solved Dad's case."

"You did? I don't know what to say." The curmudgeonly old man actually sounded choked up. "Son, that's tremendous. After all these years. Did it… I always suspected it was someone related to that boys ranch. Was it?"

Heath eased back into his seat. He should have cracked the window. Gotten a little fresh air. "It was one of their part-time ranch hands. He was using the ranch as a location to run a drug and gun ring. Dad was about to blow the case and arrest him."

His grandfather breathed over the line for a moment. "Your father would be proud."

*Are you?*

Heath propped his elbow against the window on his door. "There's something else I want to ask you. I don't really know how to ask, though."

His grandfather was silent for a minute. Heath was about to ask if he was still on the line when the man finally spoke. "Just ask, son. There's a lot of years and troubled water between us. We don't need to beat around the bush."

Heath wanted to ask what he meant by *troubled waters*, but thought it best—considering his grandfather's temper sometimes—to stick to the information he needed first. "The boys ranch was left land in the will of a man by the name of Cyrus Culpepper. However, one of the stipulations for the Lone Star Cowboy League to secure the property is that all the original residents must return for a reunion in March."

"That so, now?"

*Keep going...* "Interestingly, someone by the name of Edmund Grayson is listed among those original residents. With the same spelling and he'd be around your age. People keep asking me if it's you but I said—"

"That you'd know if your own grandfather had been a troubled youth?"

"Exactly." Heath opened his eyes; he didn't remember shutting them so tightly.

"However," his grandfather continued, "it's not surprising that you don't know a lot about me or my past since we've never been close, not since your mother refused to let my son's death be honored as it should have been and then she remarried, and that's my fault. Entirely mine."

Heath had addressed his father's murder and the boys ranch. With his grandfather still on the line, it was time to finally get answers for himself. "Why did you disappear? Dad died and you… We never heard from you again and when we tried…"

"I hung up on both you kids," Grandpa finished. "I regret that more than anything else in my life. The fact is, after that shoddy funeral she gave for your father, your mother tried to get money out of me. She said it was my fault your father died—that I put the expectation to be a cop in his head since that's what I'd devoted my life to. She refused to let me see or speak to either you or Nell unless I gave her money. And you know how bad she is with money. She would have wasted it all. You and I both know that. Not a cent would have been saved for you or Nell."

Could that be true? Heath knew his mother had been desperate but… "I had no idea."

"By the time both of you contacted me, I thought she'd gotten to you. That you were calling to ask for money as well or you'd try to get close to me with the intention of asking later on. I figured you'd hand it all over to her. Looking back, it was foolish to isolate myself. I couldn't see beyond the anger of losing my son. Guilt factored in there, too."

Heath ran his free hand over his hair. "I think isolating ourselves runs in the family."

"Oh, I hope not. I hope you're never as foolish as this old man."

"Would it be okay…" *Just ask.* "Now that we cleared the air, would you be open to the idea of us starting to get to know each other more?"

"Of course. And I'll need a place to stay in March. Can I stay with you?"

"You're coming in March?"

"For the reunion, Heath."

"Wait." Heath grabbed the steering wheel, leaned forward. "Are you telling me you *were* one of the original boys?"

"Has anyone ever told you that you're pretty slow for a Texas Ranger?"

"Lately, yes, I'm afraid I've been told that a lot."

"If it's a woman, that's the type to keep around."

Heath laughed but quickly sobered. "But why didn't I know about you being a resident here? How come you never told us?"

"I…well… I've always been a bit ashamed that I

needed a place like that to set me straight. I wanted you to see me as the state trooper who caught bad guys for a living, not the boy who very well could have become one of the criminals. I'd planned to tell you both when you were older, but then your father was murdered there and I was so ashamed to share any connection to the place where my son was killed. We stopped talking and it seemed a moot point."

"I'd love to give you a tour of the new place. They do amazing work here."

"I look forward to seeing the old and the new location."

They made plans to talk again next week, then Heath hung up. This time when he stepped down out of his truck, he glanced around and felt a deep connection to the ranch. It might not be the same location, but it was the same organization that had set his grandfather on a straight path; his father had given his life on a mission to protect the residents at the time, and it was the place where Heath had learned that he was allowed to experience joy—he could live.

The place he'd fallen in love.

Josie picked up a mini clothespin, dipped it into a bowl of white glue and then pressed it into a huge pile of gold glitter. She and Abby were inside at the large dining table making name placeholders for the upcoming Thanksgiving buffet. A few of the boys had traced and cut out hundreds of leaves on orange, yellow, brown and red card stock. The mock leaves that weren't used as name holders would be scattered down the centers of the many tables that would stretch outside for the event.

Marnie was nearby, banging around with pots and

pans in the kitchen as she prepared dinner. "You girls spend so much time and effort making things look pretty. I don't think those boys even notice."

Abby's eyes went wide. "They deserve to have a memorable Thanksgiving, and I aim to make sure every detail is taken care of so that they do."

"Suit yourself." Marnie opened the fridge and started piling ingredients onto the counter.

Josie glanced back over the instructions craft-loving Abby had ripped from one of her favorite magazines. She rested one hand on her stomach. The baby had been moving less than normal today.

Abby touched the pile of burlap she'd trimmed into squares. "I set them in order—burlap goes on the bottom, the leaf with their name written on it is glued to the burlap and then the glitter clothespin will clip on the bottom when we're done."

"If it's glued together, does it even need the clothespin?"

"I thought this out already." Abby pointed a white permanent marker at her. She was going down the guest list and writing names on the leaves with her beautiful handwriting. "With us eating outdoors, the clothespins will weigh down the cards. We don't want all of them to blow away before people can even enjoy them."

"You think of everything."

Footsteps echoed from the hall that led to the office area. Diego and Stephen were walking side by side, their heads bent toward each other, deep in conversation.

"Why do I think the two of you look suspicious?" Josie asked.

A smile blossomed on Stephen's face. "Can you keep a secret?"

"Depends on the secret." Usually secrets and rumor-spreading were discouraged at the ranch, so Josie didn't want to encourage the boys down a path they shouldn't go.

"It's one that Gabe and Bea approved," Diego said.

"Then sure."

"On Tuesday we're going to have a surprise for Heath." Stephen snatched a leftover muffin from the counter. Marnie shooed him away but looked pleased all the same. "But you can't tell him."

"What type of surprise?"

Diego bounced his way forward. "We're not telling."

Josie winked at them as they filed out of the house. She touched her stomach for the seventh time in as many minutes.

Abby caught the movement and cocked her head. "You've been doing that all day. You're starting to worry me. Is something wrong?"

Josie pressed on her abdomen again, trying to shift the baby to cause movement. Sleeping. The baby was probably only sleeping hard. Still, her heart pulsed in her temples. She *had* been feeling dizzy a lot lately.

She licked her lips. "Can you… Would you go find Heath?"

Marnie set down a pot on the oven with a loud clang and wiped her hands. "You both stay put. I'll fetch him." She crossed to the back door, tossed it open and then yelled at the top of her lungs, "Heath. Ranger Heath."

Josie sighed. *I could have gotten up and hollered.* The whole point had been *not* to cause a ruckus.

Marnie kept yelling, "Grayson. Right there. You're needed. Make those boots run."

She was so loud that Gabe wandered out of the office where he'd been meeting with Bea. "What's all the commotion?"

Heath crossed over the threshold, breathing hard. "You called?"

Gabe clapped his hands and strode forward. "Just the man I was hoping to see."

Josie opened her mouth to speak. *I called. Me! I need you.* But there were so many people gathered in the kitchen and it would feel weird to draw all the attention toward her. Especially over something medical…something she wanted only Heath to know. Too late for that.

"I have great news," Heath said, zoning in on Gabe. "I talked to my grandfather this morning. He *is* the Edmund Grayson you've been looking for and he promised to be here in March."

Gabe whooped. "One down." He reached to shake Heath's hand. "You just made my day."

Josie wound a piece of burlap around her fingers. *Speak up.* Heath wasn't like Dale; he'd want her to interrupt his conversation if she needed something, right?

Gabe pumped Heath's hand. "Tanner and I have been trying to track down my grandfather, Theodore Linley. He was an original resident alongside your grandfather." He leaned his hip against the counter and crossed his arms. "Problem is, he walked out on our family when I was eight and we've never heard from him again. His last known whereabouts was prison, but we've had no luck there, either. I wanted to pick your brain—ask your advice about hiring a PI."

Heath glanced around the room until his gaze landed on Josie. When it did, their eyes locked and everyone else faded away for a heartbeat. "Is that why I got called in here?"

Marnie slapped a dish towel onto the counter. "I called you in here because Josie said she needed you. You'd know that if you and Gabe hadn't gone straight into jawing."

Heath brushed past Gabe, sidestepped Abby and dropped to his knees beside Josie's chair. He wrapped one arm over the back of her chair and laid the other across the table in front of her. It was the closest he'd ever come to hugging her.

"What's wrong? You don't look okay." His voice was soft, intimate. In a room full of people, his words and attention were solely hers. He was doing the *Ranger thing* she'd noticed him do before—his eyes roved quickly over something…her—looking for problems, weaknesses, ways to help.

She twisted in her seat so she could place a hand on his shoulder. She needed to feel the muscles there—needed his strength to chase away her fears. The fabric was soft, worn. She leaned closer. "I haven't felt the baby move all day. I'm scared."

"When I first…? Why didn't you? I would have…" His cheeks lost some of their color and his brow creased with worry. He looked at her stomach. "Do you need me to call an ambulance? Take you to the hospital? I can carry you. That's not an issue." He started to get up.

She applied pressure to his shoulder. "No. Stay. I want you to talk."

"Talk?"

Josie grabbed his hand from the table and placed it on her stomach. "The baby moves more when you talk."

His hand was warm on her belly. His nostrils flared as he took a deep breath as if to calm down, but his eyes still looked a bit frantic. "When *I* talk or is that a royal 'you' meaning anyone?"

"You. Heath Grayson. When you talk." She'd noticed the baby kicked and changed positions more whenever he was nearby, when his voice carried. However, she hadn't planned on ever mentioning that to him. Desperate times. "Say anything."

Heath nodded and dragged some air through his mouth. "Hey…you're scaring your mom and me. Could you do us a favor and have a dance party in there?" He stared at his hand on her stomach as if he could will the baby to move.

"Just talk."

He sat back on his heels. "Let me tell you about your mama. She loves goats and baby cows, so you better be okay with that. She's beautiful. The most beautiful woman you'll ever see. Not just that, she's determined. As stubborn as a Texas summer. But it's because she cares about people so much. So don't worry about that, she—"

The baby rolled. Josie gasped. Her hand automatically went on top of Heath's. "Did you feel that?"

His mouth hung open. "I did."

Josie leaned back in her chair and closed her eyes.

Heath removed his hand slowly as he got back to his feet. "You should still call your doctor. I'll drive you over right now if he'll see you."

Josie pulled out her phone and pressed the button for her doctor.

The baby was fine. Heath was here. Everything would be okay.

# Chapter Fourteen

At the last stop sign before their turn, Heath looked over at Josie. "Are you sure you're okay to serve at the ranch? The doctor said to take it easy for a few days."

She tipped her head back and smiled up at him. "I'm not one to sit around. Besides, I don't want to miss what's happening at the ranch today."

Her hair was pinned back in a way that made her look like one of those royal princesses with their picture splashed on the front of the magazines in the checkout lane in the grocery store. The ones the internet went wild about whenever they stepped into public. Josie had the same grace and kindness about her.

He hit the button for his window, allowing chilly morning air to blast into the truck's cabin. Josie always complained about being hot anyway.

She patted her stomach. "Relax, Officer. I took it easy all weekend and yesterday, too. I feel fine. And you heard the doctor—it's only anemia. Iron supplements for the rest of my pregnancy and up my steak quota. Which—since we live in Texas—let's be honest, is not exactly an issue. I'll be good as new."

"If—even for a second today—you feel dizzy again or light-headed—"

"I know. I know." She put her hands up as if to say *Don't shoot*. "Sit down and tell you right away."

Heath tightened the grip on his steering wheel as he turned the truck past the large horseshoe-shaped metal sign announcing The Lone Star Cowboy League Boys Ranch, Founded 1947.

He ground his molars, causing a bolt of pain to blaze into his temples.

*Relax. It's not even the same location. The case is closed. Done. Get over it.*

Josie skirted a nervous glance his way. "Please tell me what's the matter. You haven't been yourself all morning."

Heath had made peace about the boys ranch when it came to his father's death. And after spending time with the boys in his detection class, and discovering his grandfather was an original resident of the place, he'd grown to view the boys ranch in a positive light. But he still had no desire to show up today.

Not on the Tuesday before Thanksgiving.

Not on the anniversary of his father's death.

"I'm fine." He craned his neck. Squinted. Up a ways near the barns...were those police cars?

"I see." She grabbed on to the door handle as they bumped down the quarter-mile-long driveway. "But that was a Ranger *fine*, which actually means something is terribly wrong."

At the end of the driveway, police cars from multiple agencies lined either side of the road. Even some of the undercover vehicles that belonged to Company F.

"Wow." Josie's whisper held a hushed awe. "So many of them came."

Did she know what was going on? Why hadn't she told him about danger at the ranch?

Adrenaline flushed hot through his veins and the muscles in his back coiled as he tossed the truck into Park. If someone had done harm to the boys or destroyed property, they would have to answer to Heath. His heart pounded. His hands shook.

If he had to—if duty called—he'd die for this place. Without hesitation.

As his father had exactly fifteen years ago, to the date.

He shoved his gun into his holster and threw open his door. "Stay here. I don't know if it's safe."

"Heath." Josie reached across the cabin and latched on to his wrist. "Take a breath. Nothing's wrong."

Couldn't she *see*? Law enforcement didn't show up in mass when everything was dandy.

He was so focused on Josie and trying to make sense of her words, Heath startled when he heard Stephen speak behind him. "There you are. I'm here to escort you to the service."

Josie let go of him and scooted out of the passenger side.

Heath pivoted to face Stephen. "What's going on?"

Red crept over Stephen's pale cheeks. "We found out that there was never a service for your dad. After everything. Your mom had a private ceremony. No big honors?"

Heath's mouth went dry and refused to form words, so he nodded, only once.

"Today we've changed that," Stephen said.

A dull ache spread through his chest. "You've what?"

Josie slipped her arm though his and place her hand on his forearm. "Come on. Everyone's waiting for you." She propelled him forward.

Rows of officers in their dress blues saluted as the three of them walked down the center of the aisle. At the front of the large gathering of people, which included all the boys from the ranch, the staff, many of the members of the Lone Star Cowboy League and a few familiar faces from around town, stood the major of Company F alongside Finn and his new wife, Amelia, and Heath's sister, Nell, her boyfriend, Danny, and her daughter, Carly.

Stephen went to stand beside Diego and Pastor Walsh.

Nell handed Carly to Danny and ran to Heath, wrapping her arms around his middle in a fierce hug. "Can you believe this?" She was crying already. "Your friends are amazing."

"Did you know?" He hugged her back.

"They told me last week, but they wanted you to be surprised."

*Surprised* was putting it lightly. Heath was overwhelmed to the point of having a hard time stringing together words.

Heath took her hand and slipped it through his arm so he had Nell on one side and Josie on the other.

Chuck, the major of Company F, made a motion for everyone to sit. "Last week I was contacted by two exceptional young men who wanted to right a wrong that had been done to one of the heroes from our very own Company F. Fifteen years ago a Ranger laid down his life while he was protecting the boys ranch and his sacrifice was never properly honored. Well, today, thanks to the dedication of his son—" Chuck gestured toward Heath "—to not let the case go cold, and to two boys—" at this he wrapped his arms to include Diego and Stephen "—who worked tirelessly to see this memorial happen, we can finally pay honor to a man we will never be able to thank enough and, moreover, will never forget."

Chuck motioned forward the honor guard, dressed in their pressed uniforms and white gloves. They marched until they were standing in front of Heath and Nell. They did an about-face and held a salute toward both siblings.

Chuck stepped down from the small stage. "Customarily we would present you with the flag from the burial, which we do not have. However—" he motioned Stephen and Diego forward "—the boys ranch was able to produce the flag that has been flying at the old site for the past twenty years."

Stephen and Diego handed a huge, faded, torn and beat-up flag to the honor guard. When they started to walk away, Heath snagged both boys and had them stand in front of him, one of his hands resting on either of their shoulders.

How could he have ever though badly of the boys here?

*God, forgive me. I misjudged this place—these kids. I was wrong.*

Chuck took a ragged breath over the microphone, evidently struggling with emotions, as well. "So you see, this very flag was flying fifteen years ago on the very day—this same day—that Ranger Marcus Alan Grayson paid the ultimate sacrifice."

In the distance, taps started to play as the honor

guard turned and began folding the flag into a perfect triangle. Taps—even when he didn't know the downed officer—always pulled at him...but being played for his father? Emotion balled and lodged itself into Heath's throat. He swallowed a few times, but it wouldn't go away. His eyes burned with tears—tears the fifteen-year-old boy had refused to shed.

The honor guard turned to attention and held the flag out to Heath. "On behalf of the great state of Texas and the Department of Public Safety, please accept this flag as a symbol of our appreciation for your loved one's distinguished service." The man pressed the flag into Heath's hands. "God bless you and your family, God bless the state of Texas and God bless the United States of America."

"Amen." Pastor Walsh took the stage. "Today we honor the sacrifice of a remarkable man, but may it also remind us that those who love God are all called to do the same. In the Bible, the book of John tells us 'Greater love has no one than this: to lay down one's life for one's friends.'"

Diego turned around and looked up at Heath. "But you don't have to *die* to be a hero, do you?"

Heath bent a little and whispered, "I don't know, son."

"I think you're a hero. I don't want you to die. That doesn't have to happen."

Not knowing what to say, Heath put his hand back on the boy's shoulder and straightened to his full height again.

The pastor stepped off the small stage and continued down the aisle. "How much more so a man like Ranger Marcus Grayson, who was willing to lay down his life for people he didn't know? Men like his son, our friend, Heath Grayson, who still answers the call by going into law enforcement." The pastor stopped in front of Heath.

*Sacrifice.*

*Lay down one's life.*

From the beginning, that was what Heath had committed to, hadn't he? He should be ready to lay down his life any second. Moments ago he'd been willing to do just that when he thought he'd have to protect the ranch.

He shifted in his boots, moving closer to Nell and placing a gap between himself and Josie.

Andrew climbed back onto the stage. "Jesus tells us that a good shepherd will lay down his life for his sheep. These men and women in uniform here today have taken a pledge stating they are willing to do that, but if you claim to be a Christian, that means you have also taken a pledge. One that says you are willing to sacrifice whatever you need to in order to honor God and point people toward Him. Please join me in prayer and then the boys have something to present to Heath." Pastor Walsh bowed his head, but Heath's ears were roaring so loud, he couldn't make out the words to the prayer.

*I've taken a pledge to be willing to lay down my life.*

Both as an officer and as a Christian.

Heath filled his lungs with a rattling breath. He'd asked God for guidance, and this was it—wasn't it? He had no right being involved with Josie. Especially not with her being pregnant. She deserved a man who would be around for the long haul. He would not allow Josie or her child to suffer another loss. Flint was right. Leaving her—letting her be so she could find another man—was the only loving, sacrificial option on his table.

* * *

After the seven-gun salute, the boys presented Heath with a box they had decorated and filled with notes each of them had written saying what they admired about him and how much they appreciated what his father had done.

Heath left her side to mingle with some of the officers in attendance, but Josie kept an eye on him. Something was off, but perhaps he was simply feeling mixed emotions because of the significance of the day and, being a man, it caused him to clam up instead of process. Even though she'd known what he was struggling with, on the drive over she'd given him multiple opportunities to confide in her, and he'd chosen not to. That hurt, but Heath seemed to need to work things out alone for a while before he spoke. It wasn't how Josie was wired, but she could respect that.

As the crowd thinned and staff members began heading back to their daily chores, Josie found her place at Heath's side.

His smile was false. Frankly, he looked exhausted. "I wanted to thank you." He didn't meet her eyes. "From the get-go you told me this was a place of healing and I didn't believe you. But you were right."

"Heath," she whispered his name and stepped closer. After the other day at Dale's grave site, where she'd prayed for God's guidance…she'd known the truth. How she felt about Heath… Those kind of feelings shouldn't be fought. They were worth every risk and danger in life.

No one else was around. *Go ahead, tell him now.*

She slid her hand onto his chest so it rested over his

heart. "Heath Grayson, you deserve to know, I think I'm falling in love with you."

"Please. Don't." As if she had sucker punched him instead of professing feelings, Heath's face fell. He stepped back, removing her hand from his chest. "Please don't say that." Anguish laced his voice. "That makes what I need to say really difficult."

Did she hear him wrong?

"I don't understand." The baby rolled. Josie hugged her stomach. "All this time. Me and you. I thought…"

"I can't be with you." The muscle that ran along his jaw popped. "You shouldn't want to be with me."

"Why not? Don't you care about me? What's wrong? Why have you been so kind if you didn't have feelings?" She was tossing out every question she could think of. "How you've been acting, it sure feels like you care."

"I *do* care," he said loudly, then lowered his voice. "But don't you see? That's why this can't ever happen. I could die today. Tomorrow. Just like my dad."

"So could I. So could all of us. I could die in childbirth."

"Don't say that."

"Please, Heath." She didn't even care if her tone came out like a whine. Every action had proven that he was in love with her. Why was he denying it?

Heath grabbed on to the fence and looked away. One of the goats trotted over and nuzzled him. He jerked his hand away, as if the goat offended him, too. "Josie, you're wonderful and you're pregnant and you deserve a man who—"

"I want you."

The goat bleated long and low.

Heath's shoulders slumped. "We can never be together. Don't you see that?"

"Is it because I'm pregnant?" Irrational, but at the moment she was willing to toss out anything.

"I can't have a family. I've always known that. I lost sight of it because…" He closed his eyes and shook his head, unwilling to go on.

She started sobbing. She couldn't even blame pregnancy emotions this time.

"Josie." His voice broke. He made a movement to reach toward her, but then fisted his hand and let it drop back to his side. "Please. It'll be okay. I just— You were right. All along. You need a man who doesn't work a job like mine. This is my fault. I shouldn't have let us get close. This is best for you. For your child."

Now there were three goats with their heads rammed through the fence links watching them.

"Are you leaving?" Josie choked out. If he didn't want her, if he wasn't in love with her, she couldn't bear being around him.

"At the end of the—"

"I think it's best if you leave. Now."

The chorus of goats bleated along.

Heath glanced down at the goats and then back at Josie. "Now?"

"Now."

"Yes, ma'am. If that's what you want."

"It is."

He hesitated, but then tipped his hat and headed straight for his truck and left. Along with her heart.

## Chapter Fifteen

Josie yawned and rubbed at her eyes.

Unable to turn off her mind and uncomfortable both because she was pregnant and because her heart ached about Heath, sleep never came last night. Not for long anyway. When Katie swung by her house in the morning to pick her up, she'd urged Josie to stay home for the day and rest, but Josie hadn't wanted to be alone.

Alone would be the rest of her life.

Sure, there would be her baby, but Josie realized that raising a child on her own might be even lonelier and more difficult than being a hermit. Her child was a blessing, of course, but a child asked questions about a missing parent. Questions that would remind her again and again that she wasn't meant to be alone. One day—a day that would come sooner than she wanted to acknowledge because that was how time worked—after her baby grew up and moved out, Josie would truly be on her own. Forever.

Because she didn't want to fall in love again. Not unless she could be with Heath.

Admittedly, Josie wasn't much help at the boys ranch

today. Diego had side-eyed her until he finally got Abby to convince her to come inside and talk. He promised to see to the calves if she stayed and visited with the ladies until she felt better.

*Sweet child.* She wanted to hug him and promise that everything would be okay. That his calf buddy would be smiling again soon. But a woman didn't just say a few words and feel better when her heart had driven off with a lawman in a truck the day before.

Josie scooped up the decorative pillow on the couch and held it to her. It wouldn't make the sharp pain in her chest go away, but it did help to hold on to something.

Abby scooted closer, wrapped her arm around her shoulders and tipped her head so their temples were touching. "I don't know what to say, but we're here. We're all here for you."

Marnie eased to the front of her chair so she could rest her hand on Josie's knee. "Maybe he'll still come tomorrow for the buffet."

Josie loosened her hold on the pillow so she could swipe at her eyes. "I told him to leave. I don't think he'll be back. I don't even know if I want him to come back."

"What can you mean, sweetie?" Marnie asked.

"I'm in love with him." Wow. That hurt to say. Would it always? "And he doesn't want me. I don't think it gets much worse than that."

Abby lifted her head. "Did he say that? Those actual words? Did he say he wasn't in love with you?"

"He didn't have to."

"Because sometimes men do strange things," Abby said. "Before John and I were married, we once broke up for a week because he decided I should be with a man who made more money since my parents are wealthy and that's how I'd grown up. Silly man. It was the worst week of my life."

"I think this is different." Josie hugged herself again. She hadn't felt this badly broken since finding out about Dale's death on the heels of his saying he was leaving their marriage. Was that how her life would be? Men leaving her?

First Dale left because he didn't think she was capable of giving him a family. Now Heath was gone because she *could* give him a family.

"He…he doesn't want a family. Because of his position. He doesn't want to be attached to me and the baby and have us face him dying in the line of duty like his father and Dale did."

Marnie picked up the teakettle sitting on the coffee table and refreshed Josie's half-gone cup of mint tea. "Well, I'm no expert in these things, but that right there sounds a whole lot like love to me."

"Him leaving? That's love?"

"No." She batted her hand. "That's plain foolishness. But the thought behind it—he cares about you and your child so much that he is willing to hurt himself in the present to save you from possible pain in the future. That, honey, is what we call sacrificial love."

"If that's love…I don't like it."

Abby moved to snag her cup of tea. "What I think Marnie is trying to say is that Heath's actions are not love—he's going about it wrong and he's confused— but the motive behind them proves his love."

"Mmm-hmm." Marnie pursed her lips. "*Confused* is a good word for that man. He somehow thinks he can tell the future and that's something only the good Lord is capable of doing. Heath's borrowing tomorrow's troubles instead of treating today as a gift. That's the wrong I see."

"Can this year just be over already?" Josie closed her eyes tightly. "I'm *so* sick of hurting. That's all this entire year has been."

Marnie clucked her tongue. "When all is said and done, don't let temporary situations allow you to question God's goodness or what He's been doing in both your and Heath's lives. I know this year's been tough on you—between Dale and finding out you'd have a baby alone and now this mix-up with Heath." She narrowed her eyes, pursed her lips and wagged her finger at Josie. "But I've watched you both over the past month. God has done great work in both your hearts. I believe He brought you two together for a very special purpose. What is that purpose? That's not for me to know or say."

"I wish it was for you to say." Josie stared at the ceiling as if she could find answers there. "It would be easier if the answers would fall into my lap."

"Maybe we'll never see Ranger Heath again. There's a chance of that. But how God moved in your heart because of that man? *That* you will always have and you're responsible for holding on to and continuing the growth that started in your heart and spiritual walk."

"The joy of the Lord is my strength," Josie whispered the verse. Putting together those lanterns felt like a lifetime ago.

Abby cupped her hand over Josie's arm. "Hold on to joy. Whatever you do, no matter what, keep holding on to joy."

Marnie rested back in her chair. "You, more than anyone here, know how fragile life can be and how quickly plans can change. We humans are finite and have no business counting on tomorrow. Which is why we have to cling to the joy of the Lord. That's not some trite saying. No, it's the only hope and only true and lasting thing in the world…the knowledge that God loves us and has sacrificed all to save us so our relationship with Him can be right. That, child, is what the joy of the Lord means."

Josie nodded, but her heart still ached. "I get that. I do. But knowing that…is it wrong to hurt about Heath still?"

"No, sweetie. It's not wrong at all. We're created to be in relationships, with God, yes, but with other people, too. I don't know what tomorrow holds, but today, today is a time to mourn for what feels like the end of a relationship that you had hoped would be more."

Josie dropped her head into her hands and let her tears fall. Abby rubbed circles into her back and started praying out loud. But Josie was having a hard time focusing.

Was it wrong to hurt more over Heath's departure than she had over her husband's death? She mourned Dale, but this was different. With Heath—pain sliced through her in a way that felt like the wound would never heal. It was more difficult knowing the man she loved was out there in the world but she couldn't be with him, than dealing with the fact that someone had passed—gone forever and there was no chance of talking to them again.

Katie Ellis charged down the hall. "I feel so bad interrupting, but something happened. Something really bad. You guys need to head to the church. Everyone belonging to the League needs to go."

Marnie was the first to her feet. "Josie, why don't you stay here? Abby and I can go see what it is."

Josie set aside the pillow and straightened her shirt. "I'm a member of the League." She lifted her chin. "I care about this ranch." She swiped under her eyes. "I'm going."

No matter what they said and despite the personal pain she was wading through, she would fight to go along if she had to. Because if Josie Markham knew one thing with certainty, it was that no matter what happened in someone's private world, life kept going. She could choose to sit in her problems, or she could get up and be a part of something and be useful in the midst of her mourning.

With God's help, she hoped she'd continue to be the type of woman who would always choose the latter.

He didn't even own a kitchen table.

Never before had Heath noticed how empty his apartment was. How empty his life really was. Not until he realized that this—his lonely, bare apartment—was his future stretching out in front of him. Years and years of this place, a fridge, a bed, a couch, TV and coffee table.

And him.

"You eat in front of the TV." He walked past his spotless fridge. No Christmas cards with smiling families adorned it. Shouldn't he have friends who'd want to send him those? At the very least? "You have everything you need."

He fished his keys from a bowl near his front door and headed outside. Nell's condo wasn't a far drive. An hour.

After everything with Josie the day before, Nell had

invited him to spend Thanksgiving with her and Danny and Danny's family. A part of him wanted to say no. Wanted to hole himself up in his apartment and shut out the world—shut out life. But he'd promised himself, promised God, this past month that he'd knock off the isolationism.

So he turned his music up as loud as he could handle without making his ears hurt and made it to Nell's in record time.

She met him at the door and thrust Carly right into his arms. "Come in. I'm so glad you could come a day early. I need you to help chop vegetables."

"Nice to see you, too, sis." He bopped Carly on the nose.

"Put me down! I have to get my ponies." She giggled, squirmed out of his arms and took off down the hallway in the direction of her playroom.

Nell chucked a dish towel at him. "I don't need pleasantries with you. Besides, I just saw you yesterday."

"Wow, you sure know how to make a guy feel loved." He rubbed his chin and dropped down into a seat at the kitchen table. There was a cutting board, a few knives and a pile of vegetables waiting for him.

Nell slipped her apron back over her head. "Love? Ha. You don't deserve to talk about love. Not after what you pulled yesterday."

"Can we not get into that?" He should have known Nell would force him to talk about Josie. It wasn't in her nature to beat around the bush.

"Oh, we can and we will. Right now." She jabbed her finger a couple times into the kitchen island so hard he felt bad for the countertop. "What on earth are you thinking?"

He grabbed a carrot. "How do you want these sliced?"

"Chopped. Cut." She threw up her hands and huffed. "Shaped into little triangles or trapezoids. Who cares? Just make them smaller and don't change the subject."

Heath grumbled and started to slice the carrots. The knife made a loud thudding sound with each cut. Might as well give her an answer. "I was thinking that I don't need Josie or her baby losing someone again and I'm a Texas Ranger. People point guns at me. People ram their cars into our trucks. People—"

"People. Die. Every. Day." Nell spit out each word as she yanked the garbage bag out of the can.

"You don't get it."

"Oh. I don't, do I?" She swung around the island to stand in front of him. Her hands on her hips. "Because you were the only one hurt when Dad died. Only you had to suffer through that, right?"

He set down the knife. "That's not what I'm saying."

"But isn't it?" She sighed as she yanked out a chair and sat down. She rested her hand on top of his. "I lost my hero, too. I know what that feels like. But you know what? I would rather have gotten thirteen years with Dad than none. And that's really what this boils down to."

"Love is sacrifice."

"Is that what this is about?" She jerked her head back in a show of disgust. "That preacher got into your head and jumbled everything around?"

He ran his fingers along the grooves in the table on either side of the cutting board. "You were there yesterday. He said loving means being willing to lay down your life."

"Yeah, I was there and he didn't just mean dying

for someone. Come on, Heath." She bumped her knee against his. "Process what you heard a little more instead of just letting fear lead you down the easiest path."

"Easy? Walking away from Josie was the hardest thing I've ever done in my life."

"No." She shook her head. "Staying and being in a relationship. Taking a risk that today may be the only day you're afforded and loving someone with everything you've got. *That* would be the harder, braver choice. Can't you see?"

"That verse he shared said—"

Nell held up her hand. "I don't need a play-by-play of the sermon. I was there. But, Heath, come on. Sacrifice doesn't always mean dying in the physical sense. Sacrifice could mean dying in your need to be the greatest Texas Ranger in the history of the world."

"I don't—"

She rolled her eyes. "Sacrifice could mean giving up anything that you're holding on to tightly—sometimes that means the shield you're using to keep everyone away or the lifeboat you've climbed into to set yourself adrift at sea." She scooted her chair closer to his. "Sacrifice could mean that you love Josie and her baby for the rest of your life and you work hard at your job but mentor those boys in your spare time and live in a way that points everyone toward the Lord."

"But that wouldn't be a sacrifice... That would be the greatest life I could picture having."

"Maybe—" she lowered her voice and looked him in the eye "—you need to sacrifice your pride. The part of you that whispers your life isn't worth squat unless you make yourself miserable and isolated and keep love at bay. Sacrifice the part of you that says you're selling out on your cause—your passion for law enforcement—if you let yourself love someone."

*Lord, help me see reason. Is Nell right? Guide me.*

Heath stared down at his hands. "I think…I think I've been living in fear my whole life. I prayed recently about it. I thought I'd let it go, but it may still have a hold on me."

She took his hand and held it between both of hers. "Things like that take a while to work through. I wouldn't expect success at letting it go to be automatic. You may battle fear your whole life. But keep fighting."

He pushed his hand against hers. "When did you get so smart?"

"I don't know. I have a pretty awesome big brother who took me under his wing."

"I love you."

"I love you, too." She let go of his hand and swatted at his chest as she rose. "But you're an idiot if you let that woman go."

"She told me to leave, Nell. Josie opened up to me and I all but walked on her heart. She might not want to see me again."

"I have a hunch she does. But…take it from a girl who had her heart stomped on before, if you're strolling back into her life, you'd best be ready to sweep her off her feet. Don't mosey back halfheartedly."

What if he'd already messed up too big? What if Josie didn't forgive him?

Heath grabbed at his hair. "She kept asking me if I was going to leave. All month. And then I did."

Nell grabbed a bowl and a spoon from her cabinets. She whirled around and pointed the spoon at him.

"Then you better do something big to show her that you're never going to leave her again. Catch my drift?"

"It's hard not to catch it when you're lobbing it directly at my head." Heath got up, crossed the room and pulled his sister into a hug. "Will you forgive me if I miss Thanksgiving?"

She hugged him back and then shoved him toward the door. "Go, Heath. Go get your girl."

Red, white, and blue flashing police lights bounced off the church's white clapboard.

Townsfolk, members of the Lone Star Cowboy League, boys-ranch staff and officers on scene all stared at the three-foot-high black graffiti marring the walls of Haven Community Church and the busted row of windows.

*Boys Ranch Was Here.*

Josie covered her mouth. "Who would do this?"

Marnie wrapped her arms around Josie and tugged her into her side. "Someone who wants to make our boys look bad."

The mayor, Elsa Wells, adjusted her horn-rimmed glasses as she pursed her lips. "We've never had something like this happen. To our church, no less. Not under my watch."

Avery Culpepper crossed her arms and smacked her gum. "My granddaddy leaves the boys all that property and assets and this is how they repay the community. Seems awful ungrateful, if you ask me. I know I would never act like this."

Fletcher Snowden Phillips—the only living relation left of the founder of the boys ranch—tipped his hat to the mayor and moved to stand beside Avery. "I've been saying they need to dismantle the boys ranch for years." He thrust his hand toward the broken windows and graffiti. "Do you know what vandalism like this does to the property value in a town?"

Tanner Barstow scowled at Fletcher. "Nobody asked for your opinion. We all know how you feel about the boys ranch. You tell us every chance you get."

"And I'll keep telling everyone until that place gets shut down and dismantled," Fletcher boomed. "I'm a lawyer."

"We know," someone in the crowd groaned.

But Fletcher didn't seem fazed. "I will find a way to sue the League. My family set up that ranch and I *will* see to it that I'm responsible for taking it down. That's a promise."

Josie turned away from Marnie and looked at Gabe, who stood next to her. "Our boys wouldn't do something like this. You don't believe they would, right? Then again," she said, lowering her voice, "we all know Heath's father was killed by a staff member. That's been confirmed now. So anything is possible."

But in her heart she couldn't believe one of the boys would harm the church.

Gabe shook his head. "This is the work of someone who wants to make the boys ranch and our organization look bad. That's all this is."

Tanner and Macy joined their little circle.

"Did you see Fletcher smirking at the graffiti? I hate to falsely accuse someone…but could he be responsible for the string of mischief we've had the past few months?" Tanner looked over at Josie. "Did Heath come to any conclusions about the thefts and calves being set loose?"

Maybe Heath had been right to suspect that Fletcher

was possibly behind the string of bad things that had happened at the boys ranch in the past two months. The lawyer had always seemed harmless, but perhaps he disliked the place enough to delve into illegal activity to ensure it would be closed down.

But Josie shook her head. She couldn't talk about Heath. She was doing her best to focus on the task at hand and that was already taking all her reserves.

Marnie rubbed a circle into Josie's shoulder. "The Ranger's gone. It's up to us to solve this puzzle now."

Gabe nodded. "Whoever did it stands to gain something by turning the town's opinion against us. We need to brainstorm. Who would benefit from our doors closing?"

Tanner angled his head closer. "Fletcher just left with Avery Culpepper to take her to lunch. Even if they aren't involved with this incident, I have to believe the two of them teaming up can only mean trouble for the ranch."

Josie finally found her voice. "Heath mentioned that some of his interviews hinted that Fletcher might be to blame for some of our troubles, but there's no solid proof."

"I'll store that information away." Gabe clapped his hands. "Tomorrow is Thanksgiving—I don't want this casting a shadow onto the festivities. How about we leave here, keep thinking of possibilities, but focus on making it a great, carefree Thanksgiving for the boys who aren't going home for the holiday. This weekend we'll all pitch in to repaint the church and replace the windows. On Sunday, no one will even be able to tell this ever happened."

Josie wrung her hands. If only Heath was here. He'd

know what to do. He might have found clues at the scene that the local police could have missed.

*Stop trying to factor Heath into everything. He's gone.*

Right… She would do as Gabe suggested.

Focus and rebuild.

## Chapter Sixteen

⟋◝

Light wind whistled through the cracked door of the horse barn Heath and Flint were momentarily holed up in. The rainstorms that had threatened to unleash a few days ago never ended up doing anything more than drizzling. Probably for the best. Rain would have meant mud and mud wouldn't have made for the best outdoor meal.

Heath tried to see through the crack in the door. He'd stashed his truck out of the way, near Flint's cabin where no one would spot it. Although, he might have been able to hide it among the fifty or more vehicles parked in the makeshift lot on the front field. Some of the boys had gone home to enjoy Thanksgiving with their families, while other families came to the boys ranch to celebrate. However, Flint explained that some of the boys were alone, so most of the staff members attended the buffet and sat with the kids without family that day.

Adrenaline buzzed through Heath's system, making it impossible for him to stay still for too long. Two baby goats—kids, as they were called—butted heads near his feet. The brown one tripped over his boot and tumbled to the ground with a tiny, offended bleat.

Heath leaned over and righted the animal. "Hush, now. You're liable to get us found out."

Outside, seventeen tables were lined in a row, heavy with place settings. Candlelight flickered from jars evenly spaced between orange and mint-green-painted pumpkins. The women had gone all out making the place look nice. Heath hoped Josie hadn't overworked herself. The thought pulled a smile to his face. Josie was bent on doing her share, so he imagined she had fought to work alongside the others.

The woman would always be a stubborn spitfire. He'd fallen for her on day one because of that trait.

Flint slapped Heath on the back. "I'm not trying to discourage you, so don't take it that way. But after everything, are you sure showing up here unannounced is the best idea?"

Heath straightened his shirt for the tenth time. "It's not unannounced. I told her I'd be here for the Thanksgiving buffet. I'm keeping my word."

Flint cocked his head and smirked.

Heath held up his hands in surrender. "I hear you. I do. Believe me. But I think doing it this way is for the best." He crossed his arms. "While we're at it, I also wanted to thank you for your warning earlier."

"The warning I gave you to stay away from Josie?" Flint picked up the white goat and held it like a football. "The one you didn't listen to? That one?"

"The very same." Heath grinned but his gut kicked with nervous energy. "And you didn't tell me to stay away—you told me to stay away if I couldn't commit. Well, I'm committed, buddy."

"So it would seem." Flint chuckled. "Are you sure you don't want to wait until you have a ring and a better plan?"

The plan was to walk out of the barn, find Josie and ask her to marry him. That was as far as he'd gotten.

"Stores are closed today." Heath shook his head. "I don't want to let one more day pass before I ask. That's the biggest thing I've learned lately—we only have today. So I plan to use it."

"I have to say, I never thought I'd live to see the day you'd settle down. It didn't seem to be your thing."

"Meet the right girl and it suddenly becomes your thing."

"That's how it tends to work for everyone else." Flint set the wiggling goat back down. It tromped off to butt the brown one again.

"Your day will come. I'm sure it will."

"Me? No." Flint pulled a face, as if he was offended Heath would broach the topic with him. "I have my hands full keeping Logan in line. I've been down that road. I'm not going down it again."

"You may change your mind."

"I won't." Flint rubbed his hands together. "But we're talking about you here. Are you ready?"

"I think it's time." Heath pulled both the goats out of the stall they'd weaseled into, holding one in each arm. "Will you pray for me?"

Flint pulled a face. "That's not really my thing anymore. Besides, even if it still was, I don't believe you'll need it."

Heath sighed. With all Flint had been through, the man had fallen away from God, hadn't he? Heath should have picked up on that before now. He should have been praying for his friend, encouraging him and talking to him about God more. He'd do so going forward. "We always need it."

"Then, sure. Although I don't believe anything I say will make a difference."

Heath took a big breath and pushed the door open with his foot.

This was it.

The mingling scents of cinnamon, nutmeg and cloves heating in the busy kitchen made Josie's mouth water. People hustled around her as she fit bowls full of baked sweet potatoes topped with brown sugar and pecan crumble onto large trays. A line of older residents who hadn't gone home for Thanksgiving waited to take the trays to the tables outside.

Thankfully, the vandalism from the day before wasn't the topic of conversation—yet. Josie prayed that the troubles they'd experienced over the past two months wouldn't overshadow all the good happening at the boys ranch.

*Please let people see the good. The positive. And please let us catch whoever is trying to make the ranch look bad. Work on the wrongdoer's heart, Lord.*

"Hot rolls coming through. Fresh from the oven. These are hot, hot, hot." Marnie held a tray above her head and bustled through the kitchen.

Bea, the director of the boys ranch, tapped Josie on the shoulder. "I think we're about set here. You can head outside and help corral people toward the tables."

Josie braced her hands on the counter and dipped her head. "Thank you, I think I'll take you up on that." A handful of them had been working in the kitchen since six o'clock in the morning, and when they weren't busy mixing and chopping, Abby had them out beautifying the tables and eating area. All of that amounted to one pregnant woman in a dress with very sore feet and an equally achy back.

Stephen slung open the back door. "Ms. Josie, I think you better come out here quick. There's something you need to see." He held the door for her and moved his hand in a circle, silently asking her to move faster.

Despite the sadness she felt about all that had happened, Josie smiled. "Sorry, Stephen, this is as fast as you're going to see this pregnant lady move today."

Stephen's grin was wider than she'd ever seen it. "I wouldn't be so sure about that."

Odd. The boy had been downright moody earlier, upset that his family wasn't bothering to come to the celebration even though, all things considered, they lived pretty close to the ranch.

Josie stepped outside and shielded her eyes from the early afternoon sun.

Diego came running up the walk. "Look! Heath's back!"

In the past, Josie had listened to people talk about moments when time stood still for them. She'd always brushed off their stories as overly sappy. She'd known love, been married and had never experienced what they were talking about. Time didn't stand still. Time moved on, dragging a person to the next second, even if they didn't want to go.

But when her eyes landed on Heath Grayson...handsome as the day was long with his wide shoulders, tight button-down and adorably hesitant smile...everything else in Josie's world faded away. The more than one hundred guests milling around the yard didn't exist. Stephen and Diego chatting about goats vanished, too. Heath cut down the yard, a baby goat bobbing under each of his arms, and headed straight toward her.

There was only Heath and Josie and for one irrational heartbeat, she wished life could stay that way. Wasn't she supposed to be angry with him?

But all she wanted to do was toss her arms around his neck and never let go.

"You're here," she breathed.

Heath's eyes took her in and his chest puffed out. "I told you I would be."

"You brought goats?" Really? That was the best she could do?

"For you. A peace offering." He lifted them up a little, but instead of handing them to Josie, he passed one to Diego and one to Stephen. "Well, *peace offering* isn't correct, either. I need to say this right." Heath stepped forward and took both her hands. "I brought those for you because I want you to know that I believe in you. I support your dream of running a successful ranch and I want to do everything I can to make all your dreams come true." His lips parted and he exhaled softly. "I'll do everything within my power to make your dreams come true for the rest of my life, if you want me to."

"The goats mean all that, huh?"

"You said you wanted goats, so I brought you goats." He took another half step closer. She had to tilt her head up to keep eye contact. "Anything you want, I aim to see that you have it. If you'll let me."

She swung his hands a little. "I just want you."

"I love you, Josie Markham. I was a fool to walk away from you the other day. I never want to spend another day without you in my life. Forgive me for being so stubborn and blind. I don't have a ring with me but I had to come and ask right away."

"Heath."

He drew as close as he could and lifted her hands so they were cradled in his, resting on his chest. "I've learned that I can't promise tomorrow, but I can promise you that I will love you completely, with everything I have, every single day the good Lord gives me. You have my life, if you want it. You are my life."

"I love you so much."

His eyebrows rose and he whispered, "Marry me?"

"Are you sure?"

He touched her hair, and his fingers slipped between her auburn strands. "I've never been more sure of anything in my life."

"Heath, I'm pregnant."

With one hand he cupped the side of her head and the other he laid over her stomach. "Let me raise this child with you. I'll be her father. I want to be there when the baby's born. Be there for both of you every day I have."

"Her?" Josie couldn't resist teasing him. Even in the midst of a special moment. "So your guess is a girl?"

His lips twitched, hinting at a suppressed grin. "Doesn't every dad want a little princess to spoil?"

Joking aside, Josie had to know. "You're willing to raise this child as your own?"

"I'll raise this child as ours, because if we're married—" he moved his fingers ever so lightly across her stomach "—this is our family. My family. I'll do anything for both of you."

Josie walked her fingers up his chest, his neck, up until she could guide his face down to hers and kiss him soundly. His arms came around her and they sealed the promise she hadn't yet answered. Because a kiss spoke louder than any words she could manage in the moment.

They might have enjoyed each other longer, but a huge cheer rose around them.

Heath and Josie parted, laughing breathlessly.

Heath pressed a quick kiss to her forehead. "I forgot about all them."

"Me, too." She laid her head on his chest. "Ranger, I know you've been slow on clues lately, so if you didn't get that one, my answer is yes."

His shoulders tightened when she said *Ranger.* "You don't mind that I'm in law enforcement? We didn't discuss that. I'm still a Texas Ranger."

"Being a Texas Ranger…that's who you are. Protective, caring, always looking for ways to solve problems. It's one of the reasons I fell for you." She circled her arms around his neck again and rose up on her toes to kiss him again. "Getting to love you is worth any risk."

Heath pressed his hands to his stomach and groaned when Josie placed another helping of corn casserole onto his plate.

She winked at him. "Oh, stop your complaining. We all know you're going to eat three more helpings anyway."

She looked so beautiful when she teased him. It took every ounce of self-discipline he possessed not to lean over and kiss her. Again. But the boys sharing their table had started grumbling after their second, or perhaps it was their third, peck during dinner, so he reined in the affection, for now.

"Besides." Stephen elbowed Heath in the ribs. He

was sitting on Heath's other side. "You can't be out of room just yet. There's still pie. And Josie even made it this time."

"For me?" Heath grinned at Josie. He couldn't stop. There was a chance he would never wipe the grin off his face. Josie loved him. He was getting married. He was going to be a dad.

"Sorry, Ranger." She pouted her lips and wagged her head. "I didn't even know you were coming."

"She made it for me." Stephen talked around a spoonful of sage stuffing. "I guilted her into it because my family refused to attend."

Heath sobered. "I'm sorry for that. Real sorry. I would have liked to meet them."

And given the teen's stepfather a talking-to. Maybe in December.

Stephen shrugged. "Whatever. I'm not letting it ruin my day." He turned to address the five other boys sitting at their table. "None of us are going to let the fact that our parents didn't show wreck today, right? There's pie and John set up hay bales in the formation of a bowling alley, and I could probably scrounge up some water balloons." He rubbed his hands together like a movie villain. "We can ambush ourselves a Ranger."

A blond boy at the end of the table stared at his plate as he pushed some green beans around with his fork. "Some of our parents can't show up. It doesn't mean they don't want to."

Josie pressed her fingers to Heath's wrist and whispered, "Visitation rights."

Heath nodded. Because of what he saw in his line of work, he'd already figured court paperwork played a role in many of these boys' lives. However, like Stephen pointed out—it was within their power to not let those circumstances affect today. After dessert, Heath would do everything he could to make certain that the boys had a good time. The hay-bale bowling alley sounded like it might be fun. He made a mental note to keep an eye on Sam and try to involve him in whatever activity Heath ended up participating in.

Heath finished the additional helping of corn casserole and then shoved his plate toward the center of the table. No more. At least, not until dessert.

He leaned back in his chair, wrapped an arm around Josie and observed everyone else at the celebration. The candles in the decorated jars wavered a little. All around them, hundreds of people mingled, laughed, shared food—all coming together to give thanks for today. And he got to be a part of it. Despite years of isolating himself, God had drawn him into a community. A community that had been waiting to welcome him—God's timing was amazing in that way.

*Thank You for blessing me, despite the fact that I was living in fear. Help me use my life to bless others now.*

Stephen laid down his fork and turned in his seat. "So I noticed that you didn't argue about the water-balloon fight—does that mean you're game?"

Heath dropped his hand onto the teen's shoulder and shook it a little. "Yes. I'm game. But first—" he pushed back his chair and offered his hand to Josie "—I'm going to take my gorgeous soon-to-be bride on a romantic walk."

Josie slipped her hand into his and beamed up at him.

Wes Corman, one of the newer residents, pulled a face. "Right now? But you two are getting married. You have *forever* to spend time with her."

Heath laced his fingers through Josie's and pulled her close. "Time's precious and not guaranteed. I have right now and I'm going to spend this moment with the woman I love." He tucked a strand of hair behind Josie's ear as her gaze captured his. "Besides, I forgot the yellow roses I was going to give you in my truck."

Stephen folded his hands on the table. "But should you have time—say—a half hour from now?"

Heath laughed. "It's yours."

\* \* \* \* \*

*If you liked this*
LONE STAR COWBOY LEAGUE: BOYS RANCH
*novel,*
*watch for the next book,*
*THE NANNY'S TEXAS CHRISTMAS*
*by Lee Tobin McClain, available December 2016.*

*And don't miss a single story in the*
LONE STAR COWBOY LEAGUE: BOYS RANCH
*miniseries:*

*Can't get enough*
LONE STAR COWBOY LEAGUE?

*Check out the original*
LONE STAR COWBOY LEAGUE *miniseries*
*from Love Inspired, starting with*
*A REUNION FOR THE RANCHER*
*by Brenda Minton.*

*And travel back in time with*
LONE STAR COWBOY LEAGUE:
THE FOUNDING YEARS,
*a Love Inspired Historical miniseries,*
*starting with STAND-IN RANCHER DADDY*
*by Renee Ryan.*

*Both titles and full miniseries available now!*

*Find more great reads at www.LoveInspired.com.*

Dear Reader,

When I first started writing this story, I knew that one of the themes would be we aren't guaranteed tomorrow. In the past week, I know two people who have passed away due to cancer. Their sudden departures made Heath's and Josie's losses all the more acute.

We only have today. That's not a trivial saying or license to "live it up" and make bad choices because life is short. Actually, it's a call to urgency.

Do you need to tell someone you love them? Perhaps there's a relationship in need of mending. Do you need to ask forgiveness or forgive someone? Who in your life needs to hear about Jesus?

We aren't promised tomorrow. Make the life you're living *today* count.

Thank you for spending time with Heath and Josie. For more fun and sigh-worthy heroes, be sure to check out the rest of the stories in the Lone Star Cowboy League: Boys Ranch series.

I love connecting with readers! Look for me on my author Facebook page, on Twitter, or connect with me through my website and newsletter at www.jessica kellerbooks.com.

Dream big,
*Jess*

# COMING NEXT MONTH FROM
## Love Inspired®

### Available November 22, 2016

## THE NANNY'S TEXAS CHRISTMAS
*Lone Star Cowboy League: Boys Ranch*
by Lee Tobin McClain

When she agrees to be little Logan's nanny over the holidays, teacher Lana Alvarez never imagined she'd start falling for his handsome single dad. Now it's up to rancher Flint Rawlings and his son to convince cautious Lana that she's on their Christmas list.

## MISTLETOE DADDY
*Cowboy Country* • by Deb Kastner

Returning to her hometown pregnant and alone, Vivian Grainger is surprised by the feelings she's developing for the gruff cowboy she's enlisted to help build her new business. Nick McKenna's never been attracted to bubbly blondes, but this Christmas he's finding himself wanting to make Viv and her baby his family.

## HER CHRISTMAS FAMILY WISH
*Wranglers Ranch* • by Lois Richer

Ellie Grant has signed on as Wranglers Ranch camp nurse to provide a fresh start for herself and her daughter. But darling Gracie wants a daddy for Christmas, and she's set on persuading Ellie that widowed dad Wyatt Wright is exactly what they both need for their happily-ever-after.

## AN ASPEN CREEK CHRISTMAS
*Aspen Creek Crossroads* • by Roxanne Rustand

All Hannah Dorchester wants is to give her orphaned niece and nephew a happy Christmas. But when the children's uncle—her ex-fiancé—returns seeking custody, can they come to an agreement—and maybe even find love again?

## REUNITED AT CHRISTMAS
*Alaskan Grooms* • by Belle Calhoune

Dr. Liam Prescott is shocked to learn his wife, Ruby, survived the avalanche he thought had killed her, but has lived with amnesia the past two years. With Christmas fast approaching, can he help her remember why she fell in love with him in the first place?

## YULETIDE REDEMPTION
by Jill Kemerer

This Christmas, Celeste Monroe is starting over with her baby nephew by moving in next door to Sam Sheffield. As they help each other overcome their scarred pasts and find peace, can they also create a family—together?

---

LICNM1116

# REQUEST YOUR FREE BOOKS!

## 2 FREE INSPIRATIONAL NOVELS
## PLUS 2
## FREE
## MYSTERY GIFTS

*Love Inspired*®

---

**YES!** Please send me 2 FREE Love Inspired® novels and my 2 FREE mystery gifts (gifts are worth about $10). After receiving them, if I don't wish to receive any more books, I can return the shipping statement marked "cancel." If I don't cancel, I will receive 6 brand-new novels every month and be billed just $4.99 per book in the U.S. or $5.49 per book in Canada. That's a saving of at least 17% off the cover price. It's quite a bargain! Shipping and handling is just 50¢ per book in the U.S. and 75¢ per book in Canada.* I understand that accepting the 2 free books and gifts places me under no obligation to buy anything. I can always return a shipment and cancel at any time. Even if I never buy another book, the two free books and gifts are mine to keep forever.

105/305 IDN GH5P

| | | |
|---|---|---|
| Name | (PLEASE PRINT) | |

| | |
|---|---|
| Address | Apt. # |

| | | |
|---|---|---|
| City | State/Prov. | Zip/Postal Code |

Signature (if under 18, a parent or guardian must sign)

### Mail to the **Reader Service:**
**IN U.S.A.:** P.O. Box 1867, Buffalo, NY 14240-1867
**IN CANADA:** P.O. Box 609, Fort Erie, Ontario L2A 5X3

**Are you a subscriber to Love Inspired® books
and want to receive the larger-print edition?
Call 1-800-873-8635 or visit www.ReaderService.com.**

* Terms and prices subject to change without notice. Prices do not include applicable taxes. Sales tax applicable in N.Y. Canadian residents will be charged applicable taxes. Offer not valid in Quebec. This offer is limited to one order per household. Not valid for current subscribers to Love Inspired books. All orders subject to credit approval. Credit or debit balances in a customer's account(s) may be offset by any other outstanding balance owed by or to the customer. Please allow 4 to 6 weeks for delivery. Offer available while quantities last.

**Your Privacy**—The Reader Service is committed to protecting your privacy. Our Privacy Policy is available online at www.ReaderService.com or upon request from the Reader Service.

We make a portion of our mailing list available to reputable third parties that offer products we believe may interest you. If you prefer that we not exchange your name with third parties, or if you wish to clarify or modify your communication preferences, please visit us at www.ReaderService.com/consumerchoice or write to us at Reader Service Preference Service, P.O. Box 9062, Buffalo, NY 14240-9062. Include your complete name and address.

LI15

*Could a Christmastime nanny position for the ranch
foreman's son turn into a full-time new family for one
Texas teacher?*

*Read on for a sneak preview of the third book in the
**LONE STAR COWBOY LEAGUE: BOYS RANCH**
miniseries, THE NANNY'S TEXAS CHRISTMAS
by Lee Tobin McClain.*

"Am I in trouble?" Logan asked, sniffling.

How did you discipline a kid when his whole life had
just flashed before your eyes? Flint schooled his features
into firmness. "One thing's for sure, tractors are going to
be off-limits for a long time."

Logan just buried his head in Flint's shoulder.

As they all started walking again, Flint felt that delicate
hand on his arm once more.

"You doing okay?" Lana Alvarez asked.

He shook his head. "I just got a few more gray hairs. I
should've been watching him better."

"Maybe so," Marnie said. "But you can't, not with all
the work you have at the ranch. So I think we can all
agree—you need a babysitter for Logan." She stepped in
front of Lana and Flint, causing them both to stop. "And
the right person to do it is here. Miss Lana Alvarez."

"Oh, Flint doesn't want—"

"You've got time after school. And a Christmas
vacation coming up." Marnie crossed her arms, looking

determined. "Logan already loves you. You could help to keep him safe and happy."

Flint's desire to keep Lana at a distance tried to raise its head, but his worry about his son, his gratitude about Logan's safety, and the sheer terror he'd just been through, put his own concerns into perspective.

Logan took priority. And if Lana would agree to be Logan's nanny on a temporary basis, that would be best for Logan.

And Flint would tolerate her nearness. Somehow.

"Can she, Daddy?" Logan asked, his face eager.

He turned to Lana, who looked like she was facing a firing squad. "Can you?" he asked her.

"Please, Miss Alvarez?" Logan chimed in.

Lana drew in a breath and studied them both, and Flint could almost see the wheels turning in her brain.

He could see mixed feelings on her face, too. Fondness for Logan. Mistrust of Flint himself.

Maybe a little bit of… What was that hint of pain that wrinkled her forehead and darkened her eyes?

Flint felt like he was holding his breath.

Finally, Lana gave a definitive nod. "All right," she said. "We can try it. But I'm going to have some very definite rules for you, young man." She looked at Logan with mock sternness.

As they started walking toward the house again, Lana gave Flint a cool stare that made him think she might have some definite rules for him, too.

*Don't miss*
*THE NANNY'S TEXAS CHRISTMAS*
*by Lee Tobin McClain, available December 2016*
*wherever Love Inspired® books and ebooks are sold.*

www.LoveInspired.com